Carrying Mason

Carrying Mason

Joyce Magnin

ZONDERVAN.com/
AUTHORTRACKER
follow your favorite authors

ZONDERKIDZ

Carrying Mason
Copyright © 2011 by Joyce Magnin Moccero

This title is also available as a Zondervan ebook.
Visit www.zondervan.com/ebooks.

Requests for information should be addressed to:
Zonderkidz, *Grand Rapids, Michigan* 49530

Library of Congress Cataloging-in-Publication Data

Moccero, Joyce Magnin.
      Carrying Mason / Joyce Magnin.
        p.   cm.
      Summary: In rural Pennsylvania in 1958, when thirteen-year-old Luna's best
friend Mason dies, she decides to move in with his mentally disabled mother and
care for her as Mason did.
        ISBN 978-0-310-72681-4 (hardcover)
        1. Conduct of life—Fiction. 2. People with mental disabilities—Fiction.
3. Country life—Pennsylvania—Fiction. 4. Family life—Pennsylvania—Fiction.
5. Pennsylvania—History—20th century—Fiction. I. Title.
PZ7.M71277Car 2011
[Fic]—dc23   2011014462

All Scripture quotations, unless otherwise indicated, are taken from the Holy Bible,
King James Version, KJV.

Any Internet addresses (websites, blogs, etc.) and telephone numbers in this book are
offered as a resource. They are not intended in any way to be or imply an endorsement
by Zondervan, nor does Zondervan vouch for the content of these sites and numbers
for the life of this book.

Zonderkidz is a trademark of Zondervan.

Art direction: Kristine Nelson
Cover illustration: Amy June Bates
Interior design and composition: Greg Johnson/Textbook Perfect

Printed in the United States of America

---

11 12 13 14 15 16 /DCI/ 22 21 20 19 18 17 16 15 14 13 12 11 10 9 8 7 6 5 4 3 2 1

For Anna Halter

CHAPTER
I

Makeshift County, Pennsylvania, 1958

My father had just pulled up to our house, the station wagon tires kicking up a spray of dirt the color of cornflakes. He hadn't even gotten all the way out of the car before I asked him. I knew I should have waited, but I couldn't help it. I had been thinking about it all day, working up my argument, practicing my tone, trying to sound older. Trying to sound stronger than my skinny, five-foot frame.

His voice took on a low, gravelly tone when he said his answer: "Girls can't be pallbearers."

I stood there looking at him through the car window, studying his face for even a hint that I might be able to change his mind. But I didn't see a clue.

Usually when Daddy raised his right eyebrow it was a sign that there was still hope I would get the answer I wanted. But not that afternoon. Daddy had made his final decision even before he heard my full regiment of reasons—and I had plenty.

"Girls can't be pallbearers. Especially skinny, scrawny girls with knock-knees."

Then he climbed out of the car. Daddy towered over me like an oak over a teaberry plant, eclipsing the late afternoon sun.

I watched him grab a small rainbow trout lying on a newspaper from the back of the station wagon. He had just come from a day of fishing up at Clay Creek, and from the looks of the measly fish and his burnt face, I didn't think he'd had a good day.

"Take this trout to your Mama and tell her I'll eat him for supper."

"But Daddy, I want to talk to you."

"Not now, Luna. I'm hot, and all I want is to get out of these smelly clothes and eat."

I hooked the trout by the gills with two fingers and carried him through the basement and upstairs to my mother. "Daddy said he wants to eat this fish for supper." I plopped the trout on the kitchen counter.

"Just one?" my mother said.

I shrugged and she looked out the window, which had a view of our backyard and driveway. "Just one, Justus?" she called.

I leaned over the sink next to my mother and saw my father raise his index finger to the sky. "One," he called.

Mama sighed. "I was counting on having trout for all of us tonight. Guess we'll have leftover macaroni and cheese." She dried her hands on her daisy-decorated apron. It was her spring apron. Mama had aprons for every season and a special one for Christmas, edged in red, with a red tieback and snow-heavy evergreen trees on the front. The rest of the months she left it laundered, ironed, and folded in a tall highboy dresser in the dining room. Every December she pulled it out like it was new, or a gift.

"It's okay, Mama. I'm not so hungry. I don't have to eat." And it was true. I wasn't hungry, not really. I thought if I had tried to eat macaroni and cheese that day it would make me upchuck. Mama's macaroni and cheese was the last thing I ate before Mason ... well, before Mason died.

Mama ignored what I said, took the trout in her left hand, and grabbed a knife from a block on the counter. She ran the knife up the fish's belly. The sound made me wince as a trickle of blood spilled onto the counter. As often as I had watched her clean fish, I was always amazed at how easily she cut near its throat, reached in with her thumb, and then pulled like she was pulling a zipper, and out came the guts, bones and all, in one fell swoop. Then she lopped the head off with a cleaver as easily as I plucked blueberries from the bush.

"How come Daddy gets the trout?" I said.

"He caught it, Luna."

She put the entrails in a small metal bucket near the back door. Mama liked to save the guts for the "night critters," as she called them. Raccoons, possums, cats, or whatever else might be prowling around out there. I was never sure who ate them but the scraps were always gone the next morning.

I heard my father washing up in the basement. "Tell him, Mama. Tell him to let me be a pallbearer."

"Hand me that cornmeal, Luna," she said like she didn't even hear me. "Think I'll fry this fish."

I grabbed the sack of cornmeal from a long, wormy shelf that at one time was the sitting part of a church pew. Daddy had nailed it to the wall so Mama had a place to keep sacks of cornmeal and flour and sugar and jars of peanut butter and a jar filled almost to the top with buttons. Seemed Mama was always replacing buttons, either on our clothes or the neighbors'.

"I'm hungry, Louise," my father called as he climbed the cellar stairs. "Lookin' forward to that fish."

"Lucky you," Mama said. "The rest of us get leftovers."

I sucked air and let it out my nose. "Tell him, Mama."

"Now isn't the time, Luna. Run that bucket of guts out to the back hedge." She pulled a half-gone macaroni and cheese casserole from the fridge. "Hot dogs. I'll boil hot dogs too."

I stood there a second or two, forcing the world to slow down long enough for me to see clearly, trying to understand what just happened. It was like they didn't care, didn't care one lick that my best friend in the whole entire world had just died and that I wanted to help carry his casket to his grave.

"Luna, the bucket," Mama said.

I grabbed the bucket and headed out back. Mama had a special place under the privets where she left food for the critters. She also hung suet and seed bells from the trees and made peanut butter treats that she tucked into the nooks and crannies of the trunks and branches like Easter eggs for the squirrels to find.

The swingset that my father built from scrap wood was empty that afternoon. Only Polly, our dog, was outside in the heat. She was a coonhound mix and the only member of the family that understood me. I still remembered the day Mama found Polly in a cave down by Clay Creek. Polly was just a pup, a few days old at the time. It seemed the mama dog had crawled into the cave to birth nine puppies. Mama brought them all home, and for a short while our house was the happiest place on earth.

Mama gave all but one of the pups away. We kept Polly on account of Mama said she looked most like the mama. Polly grew to be a big dog, brown with flecks of black fur and large brown eyes that looked like pools of chocolate syrup. She was mostly gentle, but she was also a good watchdog and barked loud whenever a stranger set foot on our property.

Polly rallied from her sun spot when she saw me. She always knew when I was thinking about something special, something painful or unusual, and she bounded over to me. I rubbed her neck and patted her sides.

"Good dog, Polly. You understand, don't you, girl?"

She whimpered and nosed my thigh. "It's okay. At least it will be, I hope."

Polly barked once. She missed Mason too. Mason was best at playing fetch with her and best at jumping into the creek and calling her in after him. I liked to watch them doggy-paddle together all the way back to the bank.

My brother and sisters were more than likely down at the creek, jumping from the Tarzan swing into the brown, muddy water to keep cool. I took advantage and sat on one of the swings. I moved back and forth slowly with my bare feet dragging in the dirt. A hot tear rolled down my cheek. I swiped it away like it was an annoying fly.

Mason had died and no one — leastways, no human — seemed to care how it made me feel.

I swung harder and harder, faster and faster, until I got the bumps. But I kept pumping my legs and pumping my legs, and I leaned way back so that I was almost lying flat and swinging, swinging and thinking, swinging and missing Mason. Swinging and thinking how much I wanted to help carry him, the way he carried me home one day when I slipped on a rock at the creek and turned my ankle. The way Daddy carried Grandpop. The way Mama carried the babies in the church nursery with gentle but firm hands. I wanted, no, I *needed* to carry Mason home.

I stayed outside as long as I could stand it. Polly lay back down — this time in the shade. But she kept a watchful eye on me. I went around to the front to avoid the kitchen and my mother. My father, freshly showered, was in the living room. He wore blue pants and a white T-shirt. The tattoo he got in the Navy of a Hawaiian hula dancer wiggled on his forearm when he snatched his newspaper from the coffee table. He sat with a thud in his easy chair. "Girls can't be pallbearers."

He didn't even give me time to ask again, so I knew I had to pull out the big guns. I called for my mother to come out of her kitchen.

"Tell him, Mama, tell him to let me be one of Mason's pallbearers. He was my best friend. I'm . . . I'm thirteen and plenty strong."

Now the thing about my mama is that she had a voice inside, a fancy voice as she called it, that told her when and when not to argue with my father. The last time Mama went against my father's final word was three months ago when my older brother, Justus

T. Gleason Junior, announced he wanted to join the Navy. Mama won that skirmish, and JT, as we called him, went off to sea. So when she put her hands on her hips and stood in front of my father, I knew she was preparing to change his mind for him.

"Now listen here, Justus T. Gleason. If you know what's good for you, you'll let Luna carry her friend's body to his grave. For heaven's sake, there ain't no rule." Then she wiped her hands together like she was wiping off dirty business and strutted back to her kitchen. Enough said.

Daddy snapped his newspaper but didn't say a word. Not a single, solitary word.

CHAPTER
2

That night, the night before Mason's funeral, I sat at the kitchen table searching every corner and every shadow of the room for words, trying to remember how Mason and I first met. I was trying to remember because his mother, Ruby Day, asked me to speak the eulogy. I thought it would be important to tell folks how we came to be such good friends. Only I couldn't remember.

Ruby Day's mind ran slower than a turtle through mud, and she was shyer than a groundhog in January. But it wasn't until she started talking and moving that you could tell something wasn't right. She had close-cropped blonde hair because it was easier to manage, an almost round face, and a tiny pug nose that tried desperately to keep her heavy glasses supported.

"I . . . I won't know what to say," she had said. "But you will, Luna. You was butter-and-eggs, remember that, butter-and-eggs?"

Butter-and-eggs. That's how Ruby Day described us. She said we were as close as butter-and-eggs, a wildflower that grew on the roadsides. It had pretty butter-colored petals and then a darker yellow in the middle, the two colors kind of running together like soft-boiled eggs run when you crack the shells.

"Don't you worry, Ruby Day," I had said. "I'll say some nice words." Even though I really had no idea what to say—not exactly. Writing a eulogy is not like writing a theme paper for school.

I mean, it wasn't all that easy to put a whole entire friendship on one piece of loose-leaf paper. He was always just there and was always my friend. Always there to teach me how to thread a proper night crawler onto my hook—something Daddy never bothered to teach me. "Girls don't fish," he said.

Mason had also been there to teach me about jazz. I remembered when he bought his first Oscar Peterson record. He looked at me with those deep brown eyes of his and a smile spread across his face wider than the record album. He said, "Jazz tells stories. Not with words, but stories just the same."

I listened real close to the music, but I never heard any stories—just a bunch of disarranged notes dancing around in the air. I couldn't catch the rhythm, if there was one. But that was okay.

I wrote down two more memories, one about fishing, the other about the time Mason fixed Jasper's bicycle. Then I erased the junk about the jazz record on account of it was just too personal to go blaring out into a crowded funeral parlor. All of a sudden, and I can't really tell why, I crumpled the page and left it there. All my memories jumbled on the kitchen table in a wrinkled ball. Then I went to bed wondering if Mama had again tried to convince Daddy to let me be a pallbearer for Mason.

It wasn't the first time I had to creep up the stairs and into my room in total darkness. I shared a room with my three sisters—Delores, who was fifteen and thought she was God's gift to us all, and the twins, June and April, who just turned five. I thanked Jesus the second I got into bed that no one woke up and asked me stupid questions.

I burrowed into the covers and started to cry again on account of the sneaky side of sadness when I saw the hall light go on. My bedroom door opened a crack.

"Go on then, Luna." It was my father. "Do man's work, but don't come crying to me if you drop the casket and that boy's body spills out on the ground."

I winced and swallowed. But I only said, "Goodnight, Daddy."

Mama was standing over me when I woke the next morning.

"I found your crumple." She held out her palm with the ball of loose-leaf on it. "Did you write anything?"

I pulled myself up and wiped sleep from my eyes. I figured I was really wiping dried-up tears that I had cried in my sleep. "I wrote some words, Mama. But it all sounded wrong. I can't figure out how to say what I want to say."

Mama sat on the bed and smiled into my eyes. "How come you loved him, honey?"

I pulled my knees up under my chin. "I don't know. He was funny and ... shy like Ruby Day, and he was fixin' to teach me how to drive as soon as he got that old heap in his garage running. He was always teaching me things, like how to swing a baseball bat. And ... and I think mostly Mason loved me back."

"Then that's what you say."

Mama stood and hovered over me for a second or two. She had her glasses on that morning, and the way the sunlight glinted through the window called attention to the blonde streaks in her mostly brown hair. And when she smiled at me it was like she was smiling into my insides. Then she reached down, took my hand in hers, kissed my palm, and then folded my fist around that kiss. "You keep that one for later. Now, I got breakfast ready. I let you sleep a little longer on account of you were up so late. Your brothers and sisters are already making quick work of the bacon, so it's probably best to eat before you get dressed. Daddy told Ruby Day we'd pick her up at ten thirty."

I heaved a sigh and swung my legs over the bed. "But, Mama," I called. "What if I mess up?"

She poked her head into my room. "You can't mess up. He was your favorite person in the whole world, and you can't say anything wrong about your favorite person."

I swiped at tears. "When do they stop, Mama?"

She scratched her cheek. "Hard to know about grieving tears, Luna Fish. But you don't want them to stop completely, do you?"

I felt my brow wrinkle as Mama headed back downstairs. *Luna Fish.* It was the nickname Delores gave me after I refused to eat a tuna fish sandwich—I'd thrown it on the kitchen floor and then slid on the mess like an ice skater when I tried to leave the table. I remember Mason laughed when I told him about it, and he said he'd have to try tuna skating himself sometime.

Mason's laugh made me think about what Mama said. I guess no tears meant no memory, and I never wanted to forget Mason—ever. So I let the tears come that morning.

By the time I got downstairs, Daddy was already in his easy chair, wearing his funeral suit—black with a white shirt and black tie. He was clean-shaven and I could smell his Aqua Velva aftershave all the way to the kitchen. Polly sat near the hearth looking all sad and concerned. I wished we could take her along and frankly didn't understand why we couldn't. She loved Mason too. I patted her head. "I know, girl. I know."

Delores was sitting at the kitchen table with Jasper, my nine-year-old brother. The twins had already eaten, cleared their places, and gone outside. I could hear them out in the yard hollering at each other.

"I think it's gonna be a hot day," Mama said. She placed a plate of food in front of me, along with a soft-boiled egg sitting in a little porcelain cup. Mama cut soldier toast as always: three strips of buttered toast lined on my plate like troops going into battle, just the right width for dipping into the egg. "So choose a light dress—ain't no rule that it has to be black."

I didn't own a black dress, and until that moment I had not given a single thought to what I was going to wear to Mason's funeral.

"No bacon?" I asked.

"I told you to hurry up. Jasper wolfed down the last four pieces."

"Pig," I said to Jasper, who scrunched up his nose and stuck his tongue out. I cracked the top of the egg with my spoon and dipped one of my soldiers into the shell, soaking up the yellow yolk, and bit into it. But the bite got stuck about halfway down. I guess I wasn't all that hungry anyway.

"You really gonna get up in front of the whole town and talk about Mason?" Jasper asked.

"I promised Ruby Day."

"How come Ruby Day ain't gonna talk?" Delores asked. "Is it 'cause she's a retard?" She crossed her eyes and screwed up her mouth. "Duh. I'm a retard."

"You shut up, Delores. Don't go talking about Ruby Day like that. Go stick your head in water 'til Mama calls you to get dressed."

Mama, who was standing near the stove, clicked her tongue. "Don't talk like that, Luna. And Delores, Luna is right—don't make fun of Ruby Day. She can't help the way she is."

"Sorry, Mama," we said together, but glared at each other.

Mama wet the corner of her dish towel and wiped stuck egg from Jasper's cheek. "Go on outside and play until I call you."

"You mean I gotta go?" Jasper dropped his fork in his plate. "I don't want to see no dead boy."

Mama put her hands on his shoulders. "Mason was everyone's friend. Remember how he always tossed a football with you? And fixed your bike chain?"

Jasper looked up at her. "Yeah, but, but—"

"Dying is part of living. Nothing to be afraid of and

you can't avoid it. Just walk up to the casket and say good-bye to Mason."

That was when Delores started to cry, but they were fake Delores tears. She had a power to turn them on and off like hose water. "Me too? You mean I gotta look at him? I ... I don't want to see no dead boy in a box, Mama. I don't."

"We're all going." She looked at the kitchen clock. "Look at the time. Now you and Jasper go get dressed in Sunday clothes."

"Yes, Mama," they said, and off they went.

"What do you suppose a dead boy looks like?" I heard Delores say.

"Probably squishy," Jasper said. "Like a fish with bulging eyes."

CHAPTER

3

I searched through my closet until I finally decided on a dark blue dress with tiny white polka dots that reminded me of stars in a night sky. Mama was right; it was already getting hot. The humidity was building, and my open bedroom windows did nothing to cool things off. There wasn't a breath of breeze outside.

My father nailed a long mirror on the back of our closet door after Delores cried and complained that she needed to be able to see her full self. I had one of my favorite poems written out in nice, neat cursive writing tacked to the door, and he just ripped it down like the words were meaningless and crumpled the sheet.

Sometimes Delores acted like she'd been crowned Queen for a Day, every day, and it made me sick to think about, because I didn't understand all that girl stuff. Still,

I stood there gazing at myself, wondering why I couldn't be as pretty as Delores. Delores had developed some shape to her hips, and also blossomed through two bra-size changes while I seemed stuck at one. My breasts just didn't seem to grow any, but hers were like mountains. Then I felt my half-slip ride down and hang about an inch below my dress. I hiked it up and used two safety pins to stick it in place.

By quarter after ten we were all assembled in the living room like it was a Sunday morning. Mama looked nice in her black dress. She wore a black hat with a tiny black veil that covered her eyes and part of her nose. She carried a black, shiny purse and stuffed it with Kleenex tissues. Then she handed each of us girls a fistful of tissues as well.

"Tuck them in your sleeve or your purse, if you've got one."

Only Delores carried a purse. "Ah, I don't wanna carry all these," she said as the twins and I shoved our tissues at her.

Mama gave Delores a swift mama glare as she tucked a Kleenex into my brother's pocket. "Just in case."

Jasper yanked his out and dropped it onto the coffee table like it had cooties. "Boys don't cry over dead bodies."

Daddy draped his arm around Jasper's shoulders and pointed him toward the front door. "Time to go, big man."

"Everybody in the backseats today," Mama said. "We have to pick up Ruby Day. She'll sit up front with me."

The twins got into the middle row of our Country Squire station wagon with Delores, while Jasper rolled over the seat onto the third seat in the very back. I sat with Mama until we got to Ruby Day's house. It was only a block away. We pulled up out front, and I started to cry again. Grief was tricky that way. Mama patted me on the knee. "You wanna go get her or should I?"

I shook my head. "I'll go."

One of the things I liked best about Mason's house was all the flowers they had growing on nearly every inch of ground. Nobody else grew as many varieties as Ruby Day. She had an uncanny knack for making flowers and trees grow. Not like Mama, who didn't have the time or the inclination to plant flowers. Their house was a small cottage complete with a white picket fence that Mason had to paint every summer—I wondered how it would get painted this year. Besides mums and irises, pansies and roses, Ruby Day had a love for purple lupines and other wildflowers. She loved them and grew them like they were really something special. There were lupines everywhere you looked.

I knocked and waited only a second before Ruby pulled the door open.

"Morning, Luna." She motioned for me to come inside.

"You ready, Ruby Day? We've got to get to the funeral home before eleven."

"I know. I know."

Ruby Day dragged her feet to the mantel. "Mr. McCullers said I could bring a picture of Mason if I wanted. Said he'd set it up on a table so ... so folks could see him as he" — she sniffed back tears — "like my boy really was."

"That's a fine idea."

Ruby Day reached up and had two pictures in her hand. "I ... I can't make my mind up on which one. You decide, will ya, Luna?"

My eyes switched from one picture to the other about nine times. Tears gathered in the corners of my eyes. "We'll take both."

Ruby might have smiled, but it quickly faded back into sadness. "That's right. Why not?"

"Ain't no rule," I said.

That morning I noticed a sour smell waft around Ruby Day, like she had forgotten to shower. "Ruby Day," I said, "where's that sweet Jean Nate cologne Mason gave you for your last birthday?"

"Bathroom."

"You wait here," I said. I went into the bathroom and couldn't help but notice that same sour smell. There was a sopping wet towel on the floor, which I picked up and hung over the tub side. I found the Jean Nate cologne in the small linen closet. It had never been opened. I opened the box as I carried the perfume back to the living room.

"Spin around," I said, and I spritzed her a few times, hoping the humidity wouldn't make quick work of the better of the two aromas.

"Can I bring flowers, Luna? Can I bring some purple lupines?"

"Have you got any picked?"

She nodded toward the kitchen. I peeked inside and saw that the kitchen table overflowed with the long-stemmed flowers. "Sure, you can bring the lupines. Mason liked them too, you know."

Once we had everything together, I helped Ruby Day into the front seat. She clung to her flowers like she was holding an infant. Mama had to squeeze real close to Daddy on account of Ruby Day being sort of a wide woman. I got in the back with the other girls and made June sit on April's lap. Then I noticed Mama discreetly pull the price tag off Ruby Day's new dress—a pretty, pale blue cotton thing with pearly white buttons down the front and a frilly white collar.

"Very nice flowers, Ruby Day," Mama said.

"Thank you, Louise. Mason likes them, too." She scratched her nose. "Hope it's okay to bring them."

"Ain't no rule," Mama said.

Daddy pulled away from the curb, and we started down Highland Avenue. The town felt eerie that morning. Not a soul outside. It was like everyone, and I mean everyone, was inside getting ready to go to Mason's funeral, or at least that's what I wanted to believe.

We drove along. I watched out the window and noticed the leaves on the trees were starting to take on that end-of-summer tired look they got come the start of school. The houses all looked pretty much the same as they always had, with porches and wide walkways leading to the front door. Some had manicured green yards protected by fences, and others were overgrown or had blotches of dirt peeking through where even dandelions couldn't bloom. All the everyday, normal stuff around me started to blur after a minute or two, and I was suddenly filled with an almost irresistible urge to scream, because a terrible mistake had been made. Mason was not dead. He couldn't be. I never saw his dead body.

I wanted to tell Daddy to stop driving and take us all home, because Mason was playing a terrible joke, like Tom Sawyer, and we'd find him sitting on our porch, just like always, tossing a football into the air. The air, suddenly there wasn't a molecule of oxygen left, like some ugly giant stood over our town and sucked all the breath right out of it. I pulled at my dress collar as sweat dripped down my face.

"Gimme one of those tissues," I said to Delores.

She opened her purse with a snap. "Here. You're sweatin' like a pig, Luna."

I saw Daddy glance at me in the rearview. His eyes

crinkled and I noticed tiny wrinkles. "The funeral home has air conditioning, Luna Fish. You'll be all right." I stared out the window, debating whether to scream or not, and thought better of it once Daddy pulled into the Hazleton Funeral Home parking lot and a short, stubby man slapped a magnetic orange flag on the fender. Because at that moment I knew with all my heart and all my soul that a hole had been ripped in the Milky Way.

CHAPTER
4

Ruby Day shifted the lupines into the crook of her right arm and linked her left arm with mine as we entered the funeral home. We were both shaking from head to toe like two quaking aspens in a storm. My knees had turned to jelly somewhere between Highland and Colton Street. Ruby Day squeezed my arm. "It's gonna be okay, Luna."

"Thank you, Ruby Day. We're both gonna do just fine. Fine as a gentle spring rain."

The funeral was scheduled to begin at eleven, and we got there about ten minutes before—time enough to set Mason's pictures on the guestbook table and take a few minutes to be alone with Mason. Mama kept our family in an outer room while Ruby Day and I said good-bye.

If anyone would have told me that I would be standing there in front of Mason's dead body, I would have laughed and said they were crazy. If anyone had told me that Mason would get hit by a truck and be killed, I would have laughed even harder. Mason was like the safety monitor of the whole world. It seemed like he was born wearing one of them yellow safety-monitor belts, always telling me to be careful and reaching out his hand to help me off a log or over rocks when we went exploring down at Clay Creek. But none of his safety monitor skills did any good when it mattered. It was raining and Mason decided to head down to the music store and buy a new record album. He saved quarters for months to buy it. Mason especially loved piano jazz and was head-over-feet for Oscar Peterson.

The night Mason died was eerie and foggy. The few streetlights in town were shrouded in low clouds and illuminated nothing more than a few feet of air and sky. Mason had ridden his bike down to the five-and-dime, and, as far as the sheriff could reason, he hit a bump or a rock or something and skidded on the slippery road into the path of an oncoming livestock truck. Doc LaSalle said Mason died instantly—never knew what hit him. Except, standing there in front of him in the funeral parlor that morning, I believed with all my heart that Mason saw the truck and just couldn't stop himself. Imagine that, the last thing you see in life being the headlights and grill of a truck full of chickens headed for market.

I thought the sight of him in a casket would be a whole lot more upsetting. But, at that moment, it was like he was reaching out to me from heaven and telling me he was doing good, and that God had more jazz albums than the five-and-dime store.

They'd dressed him in a blue suit that looked big on him, with a white shirt and dark blue tie. If Mason had known he would have given them what for—for sure. He would have said, "Mr. Undertaker, I ain't wore a suit in my whole life, and I ain't wearing one to my grave. You put me back in my blue jeans and my flannel shirt and I'll be just fine."

"They got that suit from the back storeroom," Ruby Day said, reading my mind. She reached into the casket and touched his face. "They got loaners."

My eyebrows lurched when she said that. "Loaners? But, but—" I stopped talking. I didn't want to conjecture at that point, knowing how Ruby Day got facts mixed up.

People, including kids from school, started to file past and then greet Ruby Day and me and tell us how sorry they were for our loss.

"Is my dress okay?" Ruby Day whispered to me. She still clutched the lupines. "I . . . chose it on account of Mason likes blue."

"It's a fine dress, Ruby Day." And I kissed her cheek.

The high school football team showed up in suits and ties. I'm sure Coach Trawler made them dress up. They stood at the back of the room the whole time like some kind of honor guard. They all had black armbands with Mason's football number painted on them—number ten. They must have been sweltering inside them neckties.

I ached for the service to start, just so I could get it over with for them and for me.

Sad organ music drifted out of a record player in the corner of the room. I should have brought one of Mason's record albums with me. I held Ruby Day's hand while Pastor Davis gave a short sermon and then signaled for me to give my eulogy.

I really didn't have much to say. I stood there for a few nervous, silent moments looking out over the faces of nearly the whole town, waiting for inspiration or for someone to put me out of my misery. Then I remembered what Mama said, and I just started to tell the people why I loved Mason.

"Mason was my best friend. He taught me about music. Jazz, mostly. He especially liked this fella named Charlie Parker, and Oscar Peterson. He loved that piano playing. That's what he was going for that night, the night he"—I swiped at tears—"died." I swallowed. "Mason taught me how to thread a proper worm on my fish hook, and he was fixin' to teach me to drive." I looked at Daddy. He smiled a little.

"Mason was good to his mama. He helped her all the time. He never said nasty words about anyone and always wiped his feet on the mat. Not many of you know this about Mason 'cuz he liked to keep it secret, but Mason liked to write songs—poems, about the sun and the stars and his mama."

I looked at Ruby Day. She was bawling her eyes out as Mama held her hand.

"But mostly," I said at the end, my eyes looking at my feet and tears dripping down, "Mason listened to me and never made me feel like I didn't matter. Mason never made anyone feel like they didn't matter, especially his mama, Ruby Day."

I looked up in time to see, and hear, one of the football players, Clovis Hunkle, cough the word *retard* into his fist. Of all the folks there that day, Clovis was the one that stood out. He and Mason hated each other, and more times than not wound up in a fight, with Clovis trying to beat the snot out of Mason until someone came along to break it up. He only went to Mason's funeral because the coach forced him to; I was certain of that.

Coach Trawler, the gym teacher, hauled Clovis out of the room by his ear.

That was that.

Mr. McCullers stood at the front of the room looking very grim and serious. More serious than I wanted him to.

"Thank you, Luna," he said. And then he motioned for me to return to my seat.

The organist began to play another sad-sounding hymn. I think it was called "In the Garden." I recognized it from church. We were supposed to sing along, but I couldn't get a note to come out.

After the song, Mr. McCullers said, "At this time I would like to ask the pallbearers to come forward."

The six of us—Daddy, three members of the football team, and Coach Trawler—stood and moved in a horizontal line like a small tide toward the casket. My stomach went wobbly. Mr. McCullers indicated with a sweep of his hand that we should stand like a wall in front of Mason. Next, he slowly lowered the lid. I swallowed and had to close my eyes. They opened just as the last touch of sunlight rested on Mason's face.

"Good-bye," I whispered. And then it was done. The coffin was closed up tight. But I liked to think that the little bit of sunshine stayed inside.

Even with my back turned I knew I heard Ruby Day crying hard. I was doing all right, hanging tough. No sobby tears.

"This is it, Daddy," I said. "Time to carry Mason."

Daddy nodded. "Come on, Luna Fish. You're gonna do great. Just make sure you get a good grip."

Mama took Ruby Day's arm. "We'll just wait in the car."

I held on tight to the casket exactly how Daddy told me and prayed to God that my palms wouldn't go all sweaty. Us six pallbearers carried the coffin to the hearse first and then clear across the cemetery field to a little section called the Lamb's Garden. I sat with Ruby Day and held her hand until Pastor told us to leave a flower on the casket. Ruby Day dropped her bouquet of lupines into the hole and then stared down after them like she had just made the biggest mistake of her life. I gave her a little tug on the shoulder.

"You did right, Ruby Day. Let them go."

"It was a good year for lupines, Luna," she said. "A real good year."

CHAPTER
5

Daddy pulled up in front of Ruby Day's house. Mama kissed her cheek. "You be sure and call if you need anything, anything at all."

Ruby Day could barely nod.

"Mama, could I sit awhile with Ruby Day? I can walk home later."

Mama and Daddy swapped glances that made me think they had some deep concerns about me spending time with her alone, but I shrugged it off. They didn't really know her the way I did. There had been talk about having a luncheon, but Ruby Day didn't want that. She said it would be better if everyone went home right after the service. If you ask me, I'd say Ruby Day just didn't want the fuss.

"Well, okay, you go on," Daddy said. "But be home in time for supper."

Ruby Day stepped out of the car and was waiting on the curb, clutching her pictures of Mason like babies.

"And Luna," Mama grabbed my arm before I could get out of the car. "If she gets to be too much, you give me a call, okay?"

"Okay, Mama."

I followed Ruby Day into the empty house and watched her gently place the pictures of Mason back on the mantle. She let her fingers linger a second or two on each picture, lightly touching Mason's cheek. That was when it struck me—Ruby Day would be alone in that house for the rest of her life. Without Mason around to take care of things, Ruby Day could be in a frightful bit of danger. She wasn't very good at remembering to turn off the flame under a pot or close the windows during a storm. She'd forget to go to sleep at night and would sit up watching television unless Mason stopped her, and she was forever losing her house key. Mason distributed six keys under six rocks in the garden and marked each one with a little white dot. Three of them had been turned over already.

"I can make tea," Ruby Day said.

The heat of the day had really started to build and the last thing anyone needed was a hot drink. "How about iced tea, Ruby Day? You got iced tea?"

Ruby shook her head. "I ain't made any since ..." Then she looked at her shoes—a pair of white Keds with blue laces.

"I can make some. Mama showed me how, and you know Mama makes the best iced tea in Makeshift."

"She rightly does, Luna."

Ruby Day followed me into the kitchen, where I started to boil a pot of water.

"Now, as soon as that starts bubbling, we'll drop in the tea bags and let them steep."

"Okay, Luna." Ruby Day had her hands locked in front of her on the kitchen table. "I miss him, Luna. I miss Mason."

"So do I, Ruby Day. So do I. But you know, I bet Mason is looking down on us right this minute."

"But that ain't possible, Luna."

"Well, you know about angels, don't you, Ruby Day?"

"I don't believe in angels. They's just fairy tales."

She ran into the living room and stood there shaking with her hands balled into tight fists. Then all of a sudden, like a rattlesnake strike, she pulled her glasses off and threw them onto the couch. Her eyes turned so tiny they startled me. "Mason ain't nowhere." Ruby Day started to shriek like I never heard her. She sounded like a great blue heron the way the sound came from deep in the back of her throat.

I grabbed her shoulders. "Ruby Day. Ruby Day. Stop it." I shook her slightly but she kept shrieking. I shook her harder while I fought the temptation to slap her face. The shrieks came louder until I couldn't help myself and pushed her onto the couch. She fell with a thud and cried.

"I'm sorry. I'm so sorry." I tried to hold her but she wouldn't let me.

"Just go home, Luna."

The sour smell was back and I had to ignore it. "No, Ruby Day. I can't leave you alone. You've got nobody to take care of you." And the second the words left my mouth, I knew I shouldn't have said them, because Ruby Day let out another shriek. But then it stopped and she let me hold her for a few moments.

"I bet the water is boiling. What say we go make some iced tea."

Ruby jammed her glasses onto her face. "Okay, Luna."

I placed seven tea bags in the water with their tags hanging over the side like tiny shirts left out to dry. "In a little bit we'll add the sugar and the lemon, then some water, and … bingo. Iced tea."

Ruby Day swallowed. "I am thirsty, but right now I think I'd like to go get on my gardenin' clothes and go out to the back with the lupines."

"Sure, Ruby Day. You go get changed and I'll finish up the tea."

I looked around the kitchen. I had been in the room about a gazillion times. I opened the cabinets and all I saw were a couple cans of Campbell's chicken noodle soup, spaghetti, and graham crackers. Ruby Day had precious little to eat. The more I wandered around the house, the more I realized that Mason had been taking care of Ruby Day like she was the child for nearly his whole life.

Mason never talked much about his father. Actually, Mason never, ever talked about him, and all I knew was what Mama told me. Ruby Day's husband died when Mason was only a tiny baby. And then, Mama said that all she knew was, "Ruby Day and Mason lived with Ruby Day's father until Mason was seven years old—that was when her father died and they moved to Makeshift." But that's all anyone knew for sure.

Mason'd been caring for his mama ever since. I just didn't understand it until that day. She really couldn't take care of herself—by herself. She needed help. Mason did tell me that Ruby Day's Uncle Charles would show up every now and again and check on them. But even so, Ruby Day needed everyday help.

I tossed the tea bags into the trash, added the sugar, and fortunately I found a bottle of ReaLemon Juice in the fridge and poured a tablespoon into the mixture. Then I added some ice and dumped it all in a pitcher, added cold water, and poured two tall glasses of iced tea.

Ruby Day was out back tending to her flowers, and I watched from the kitchen window. She squatted on her bare heels, rocking back and forth like an old lady. I imagined her thoughts were so heavy she could barely lift her head under the weight. The sun, now on the down side of her journey, cast long shadows of Ruby Day's flowers onto the grass.

I snatched a sun hat from a nail near the back door, stuffed it under my arm, and stepped outside carrying the two glasses of iced tea. The glasses began sweating from the collision of heat and cold, small droplets running down and onto my wrists, cooling them.

"They get bugs this time of year," Ruby Day said. "I can pick most of 'em off." Ruby Day was sweating in the sun. She wiped her forehead with the back of her gloved hand.

"Here you go, ice-cold tea. Sweet, the way you like it."

Ruby Day took the glass, sipped, and then set the glass on the lawn. "Thank you, Luna."

I crouched down and tied the wide-brimmed hat onto her head. "Don't want to get sunstroked, Ruby Day."

She looked up at me, squinting. After a few seconds she let go a thin laugh. "I always forget my hat." Then she went back to picking aphids off the purple flowers like I wasn't even there anymore.

I stayed at Ruby Day's house for a little while longer. I washed the few dishes in the sink before I noticed an odd, mildewy smell coming from the laundry room — actually a little service porch off the kitchen. I opened the washer and the odor hit. Wet clothes that must have been there since the day of Mason's accident. I added more detergent and started a second washing. Then I ran the vacuum and dusted the living room, making sure to pay close attention to the pictures of Mason that Ruby had scattered all around the room. I will admit it was hard, and I shed tears as I went along, but by the time I finished I knew I was faced with a problem that I didn't think anyone else in Makeshift County was thinking about: What would come of Ruby Day?

CHAPTER
6

I left Ruby Day just before dinnertime, even though I was feeling a frightful amount of worry for her staying in the house all night, all alone, after she just buried her only boy. The thought made me swallow about a dozen times before I hugged her tight.

"Now listen to me, Ruby Day. You watch TV until ten o'clock and then go to bed." I looked her square in the eye the way Mason always did when he needed her to understand. "And if you cook anything, make sure you turn the flame off when you're done or you could burn down your house."

She swiped at tears. "All right, Luna. I will."

All I could do was stand there and heave a great sigh, feeling like a whole mountain of burden had just been dropped on my shoulders. Ruby Day was suddenly completely alone, and I couldn't stand the thought.

I walked home thinking and thinking about Ruby Day batting around her house with nothing particular to do now that Mason wasn't there for her to tend to. I imagined her sitting on the couch watching cartoons and forgetting to eat, forgetting to wash up, maybe forgetting to breathe now that her son was with Jesus. I looked to the sky as a lacy cloud skirted by. For a minute I thought I saw Mason's smile.

Mama was preparing one of her cold summer-day meals for supper. She hollowed out cantaloupes and filled them with fresh fruit. Then she made ham-and-cheese sandwiches and that was supper.

Daddy had gone off to work after the funeral so he wasn't there. He and the other plumbers were laying a new water service near the new houses they were building behind the high school. Daddy said it would be good summer money, enough to maybe make a real family vacation possible. We all cheered when he said it. Even Polly Dog, who was sitting as close as she could to me, let go one of her happy barks. When Polly sat on her haunches the top of her head reached my kneecaps, so I could easily scratch behind her ears. She liked that best of all.

Most of the men in Makeshift worked the coal mines, following their daddies into the deep earth. But not my daddy. He said some men needed to stay on top of the world to take care of things that needed taking care of, like toilets and pipes.

"Luna," Mama said, "how's Ruby Day?"

I shook my head. "She ain't good. She's just pretendin' to be good."

Mama took my hands in hers. "Sometimes pretending is a good thing. Before you know it, you ain't pretending anymore."

I pulled my hands back. "I need to get out of this dress. I'll be down to help in a minute."

Mama looked at me with needle-sharp eyes that cut right through. "You got somethin' on your mind, Luna."

It wasn't a question.

"Maybe, Mama."

But I didn't tell her just then. I went to my room where Delores was sitting at her vanity table primping herself like always.

"You can keep trying," I said, "but no amount of powder is gonna change your pig nose."

Delores looked at me in the mirror. "I hate you, Luna." She tossed a bottle of something, I didn't know what, at my head. It hit the wall.

I pulled a pair of shorts out of my drawer and looked

at Delores. I had no right to say what I said. It was jealousy that made me say mean things to her, since Delores was so pretty. "I'm sorry, Dee," I said. "I'm sorry I said you had a pig nose. I don't wanna fight anymore."

She glared at me in the mirror.

I changed into shorts and a light, cottony blouse, which I tied across my midriff to be cooler.

"Daddy'll make you untie that shirt, you know."

"I know. But he ain't home yet."

The twins bounced into the room with basketballs.

Delores banged her brush on the table. "Can't I ever get any privacy around here?"

I tried to shoo the girls out but they refused and started jumping on their beds.

"Stop it," Delores screamed. "Just stop it now or I'll tell Mama."

April stuck out her tongue.

"Maybe Daddy will finish that basement room he's always talking about," I said.

That garnered nothing more than another glare from Delores. She was right. No one believed Daddy would ever finish the room.

The twins tired of bouncing and left carrying their dolls—one with knotted-up hair and dirty clothes and the other with long, silky strands and a neat dress. The dolls always made me think of Delores and me.

Mama and I finished preparing fresh fruit—strawberries, cantaloupe, honeydew, blueberries, apples, bananas, and one mango that Daddy got as payment for fixing Grace Pickler's leaking faucets. Mangoes weren't readily available at Haskell's Grocery Store, and Grace claimed she got it from a visiting missionary on furlough from South America. We filled the cantaloupe bowls once everything was cut. I stole a taste on account I never saw a mango in my whole life. It was sweet and juicy, and, as I held it in my mouth, for a second I was an exotic firewalker.

"Daddy will be home any second," Mama said. "You better untie that blouse."

I swallowed. "Fine. But I am nearly fourteen years old—old enough to make my own fashion choices, and besides, it's hotter than ... than jumpin' blue—"

"Careful, Luna," Mama said with a smile and raised eyebrows.

"Jumpin' blue heck, Mama. I was gonna say jumpin' blue heck."

"Uh huh, now get out the ham and cheese and mustard, and grab that bag of chips from off the refrigerator."

"Why's Daddy always tossing them up there?"

"Been doin' that for years."

I opened the bag and dumped the contents into a large pottery bowl. "At least you got help."

"What's that supposed to mean?"

"I'm sorry, Mama. I'm just worried about Ruby Day and I miss ... I miss Mason so much I don't think I can stand it." Mama moved toward me and pulled my hair back, tying it into a ponytail with a rubber band she had around her wrist. "The heat is making us all cranky, and it's been a hard day."

Tears welled in my eyes. "I miss him. I miss him so much."

She pulled me into her chest. "I know, Luna Fish. He was your friend."

"But why? Why did God take him? Why would God take a young boy—fifteen, and with a retarded mother and all. Why?"

Mama patted my head. "I don't know, honey. Those questions cannot be answered on earth."

I pulled away from her when I heard the station wagon pull into the driveway. "Daddy's home."

The kitchen table was crowded with food and people with arms in constant motion passing this and that, eating and slurping juice from the cantaloupe bowls. My whole family was gathered like it was an ordinary day. Well, all except for JT, who was off on a ship

49

somewhere in the Mediterranean Ocean. I wrote him a letter and told him about Mason, but I figured it could be a few weeks before I heard anything back.

Jasper slipped Polly a piece of honeydew melon. She dropped it on the floor and I gave Jasper such a look that he reached down and picked it up. "Sorry," he said.

"That's right," Mama said. "Polly doesn't eat much fruit."

I ate a few bites of my own fruit, but it wasn't going down easy.

"Mama, Daddy," I said as I pushed my plate away. "I got something to say."

"Say it, Luna," Daddy said. He sipped coffee.

"You got all these kids around the table, right?" I said.

"Yeah, that's right," Mama said. "And I love each one of you equally."

"That ain't it," I said. "It's just that ... that—" I threw my napkin into my cantaloupe. "Ah, never mind."

"What is it?" Daddy said. "I had a long hard day in the sun so I ain't in no mood for games. Just say it. Haven't I always told you to just say what's on your mind instead of lettin' stuff fester like a boil that pops when no one expects it or wants it?"

"Yes, Daddy."

"Maybe I should excuse the children," Mama said.

"Ah, phooey," Jasper said. "We wanna stay and hear what Luna says."

Mama looked at me for a long few seconds. "No, I think Luna's got something important stuck in her craw. You kids go on upstairs. I'll call you down for ice cream."

After a few minutes of screeching chairs and weak protests, the kids, including a disgruntled Delores, were gone and I sat face-to-face with my parents.

"Okay, I'm just gonna say it. Just the way Daddy told me Mason was ... was gone. He just said it, no hems or haws, just came right out and said it."

Daddy laughed. "You're hemming and hawing."

"Okay, here goes." I sucked nearly all the air out of the kitchen. "I think I should move in with Ruby Day and help her now on account of Mason being ... being gone, and she don't have anyone to take care of her, and she can't live alone." I took a deep rescue breath and let it out slowly. I had plenty of time to breathe. My parents looked at me like I had just that second sprouted onions out the top of my head.

At that moment Delores came bounding into the kitchen. "I think that's a great idea. Just think, one less bed in our room. I could get my own dresser and more closet space and ... and—" She nearly swooned.

"Delores Mae Gleason." Mama stood from the table and took three steps toward my sister before Daddy pulled her back. "Steady, girl."

"Delores Mae Gleason. You were eavesdropping. What have I taught you about eavesdropping? It's despicable. Now go to your room and don't come out until I tell you and ... and do not, I repeat, *do not* tell your sisters and brother about this."

"Well, it is a good idea," she said and then skipped off.

The thing about Delores is that she had a selfish streak running down her back like white on a skunk, and she was about as surly and conceited as anyone could get. Claimed she was going to go to Hollywood one day and become a famous actress.

Mama sat back down at her place at the table. "Luna, I ... I don't know what to say. I can't believe you would even ask that question. I had no inkling that you were thinking like this."

"Well, it ain't like I've been thinking long and hard, Mama. The idea just struck me today while I was with Ruby Day."

"But we're your family." Mama's eyes went wide.

"I know that. It's just that Ruby Day has no family anymore."

"So you're gonna just move on in and become Ruby Day's family, take Mason's place?" Mama stood and started to clear the table. She piled plates on plates and brought them to the sink. "Whose turn is it for dishes t'night?"

"Delores's," I said. "And this time she better not let Polly lick them clean. She needs to wash them."

Mama started heaving cantaloupe rinds into the

trash. "Make certain this trash gets outside t'night, Justus. In this heat it'll stink to high heaven by mornin'."

Daddy looked at me and put his finger to his lips, like he sensed I was about to say something. "I'll make certain, Louise."

Then he directed his attention to me. "You go on now. Let your mama and me discuss this. You dropped quite a bomb on us, you know."

"I know, Daddy. But ... but Ruby Day can't live all by herself."

Mama swallowed. "Well, that ain't our responsibility, Luna. She's got to have family somewhere."

I shook my head because no one cared for Ruby Day like Mason.

Mama pushed her fruit-juicy hand through her hair and grimaced when she realized what she'd done. "Just go on outside or upstairs, Luna. Please. Just go."

CHAPTER

7

I stood in the living room trying to listen in on their conversation. But that didn't last long. Daddy shooed me out so fast my head spun. Instead of going upstairs to meet the usual wrath of Delores, I headed outside to sit on the porch swing.

The sun was finally starting to set, which meant the temperature would be dropping even though the humidity would stick around like a mean sister. And I mean stick. It was like being wrapped in a smothering blanket all summer long. The only relief we got on days like those was from swimming down at Indian Head Rock or sometimes from the hose when Daddy said it was all right. Mason and me spent lots of hours at Indian Head, jumping feet first from the old rock and floating on the creek.

Once in a while Ruby Day would come with us. She liked to wade out just to her knees and splash the water at us. She laughed and laughed like it was the best trick ever. Maybe I'd take Ruby Day to the creek.

"You really gonna go live with Ruby Day?" It was Jasper. He'd snuck into my peripheral vision while I wasn't looking. "Don't you like us anymore?"

"It ain't like that."

He sat on the porch step. "Then how come?"

"Because Ruby Day needs me. There ain't no one else."

That was when Mama appeared at the screen and called me back inside. I tried to read her face when I passed by her on my way to the living room, but I couldn't. Mama could keep a secret like nobody's business. I sat in the rocking chair on account of I figured rocking could keep me busy while my parents said their piece.

"You're only thirteen, Luna. Too young for so much responsibility," Mama said.

"But Mama, you were just seventeen when you and Daddy got married, and Clara Greely down the road is fixin' to marry that boy, Hugh, come September as soon as he starts in the mines."

"That's different."

"But she's just sixteen. Her daddy said it was for the best on account of they can't afford to feed all the mouths they got."

That was when Daddy spied Jasper hiding behind the sofa.

"You come out of there," Daddy called.

Mama shooed Jasper away. "Go on now, boy, find something else to do. This ain't your beeswax."

"Don't go, Luna," Jasper said.

"I'll just be down the street. I'll see you all the time."

"You heard your mother, Jasper. Now git!"

Mama patted my knee. "What about your dreams, Luna? What about going to college and becoming a teacher?"

"I can still go," I said. "I'll just go close. I can drive back and forth every day." I turned to Daddy. "Daddy, you and me can get Mason's old jalopy running good enough."

"I don't know, Luna." Mama shook her head.

"Please, Mama. You'll see. I'll become a teacher and make enough money to care for myself and Ruby Day, even though she gets money from her job at the grocers and ..."

I stopped talking because right then I didn't really know where she got her money. Mama's brow wrinkled. "Come to think of it, she just has that little job bagging groceries, and that can't pay enough."

"Yeah, but she works harder than anyone I ever seen down there, Mama. She's a right good bagger and Mason told me she never broke an egg or a jar or—"

Daddy finally piped up. "Look. It's all fine and

dandy that you still want to go to college, but how can you be so sure Ruby Day even wants you to come live with her?"

I hadn't thought of that. "I guess I don't know for sure, Daddy. But ... but I can't imagine one reason why she'd say no. She's got to be mighty lonely in that house."

Daddy walked to the stairs and stood with his hand on the stair rail and one foot on the first step. "I can't be giving you much money, Luna. Maybe a little here and there, but you'll be on your own if you do this."

"She can come home for meals sometimes —" Mama patted my knee again and pulled me close. "I suppose I can bring you some plates on occasion — you know, fried chicken and fish."

My chest swelled like it was all of a sudden filled with the air it had been missing since Mason died. I took such a deep breath I got dizzy for a second. "You mean it, Mama? I can go?"

"Pack your things."

Mama swiped at tears in her eyes. "I love you, Luna."

I touched her cheek. "I love you too, Mama. You'll see. I'll be fine, just fine, and I'll become a teacher. A great one. You'll see."

"Okay. I know you will."

When I walked into my room, I saw Delores wearing a white slip and sitting at her table primping.

"What are you getting all dolled up for?" I asked.

"None of your beeswax, pig nose."

"I bet I know. You're running out to meet Carl Yeager."

She turned suddenly and threw her brush at me, barely missing my left ear. "I am not, and besides, even if I was, what's it to you?"

"Ain't nothing to me, especially now."

"What's that supposed to mean?"

I opened my two drawers and pulled out all my clothes, dumping them on my bed. "Seen that old suitcase April and June were playing with?"

"Yeah, they filled it with doll stuff and April said it got lost in the creek. They were using it for a boat."

"Shoot! I need that." I looked around. "I'll just use cardboard boxes then."

"Where you—" She stopped and stared at me. This time face-to-face, not face-to-mirror. "You mean Mama and Daddy are lettin' you move in with Ruby Day?"

"Yep. I'm goin' right now, so it looks like you'll be getting those extra drawers."

Delores pretty much leaped off her chair. "No foolin'? You're really going?"

"Yes. Mama said to pack my things."

Delores sat back down with a thud. "I don't believe it. How come you wanna go live with a retard, anyway?"

"I told you not to call her that." I dumped a box full of doll heads and toy trucks onto the floor. "This'll do."

"But that's what she is. How come you wanna live with her?"

"Because she doesn't have anyone else." I watched Delores watch me in the mirror, and for a second I thought I saw a tiny hint of compassion cross her brow.

"You'll be sorry." Delores finished her makeup or whatever she was doing and pulled on a light pink seersucker dress. Then she checked out the view in the mirror. "Don't wait up," she said with a wave of her hand. "Oh, guess you won't be here when I get home."

"Nope. I'll be at Ruby Day's if you need me."

"Need you? Why would I ever need you when I got Carl?"

That's what worried me. But I never told her that. Delores was the type that went against things she was told just for the sake of doing it—and usually without a thought to the consequences. Mama said she was like a whirling dervish going every which way without a thought to what was in the path.

I finished gathering everything I thought I would need. "It'll be better now," I said, standing at the door looking in.

Mama and Daddy were sitting in the living room when I came down with my box. Mama was sewing a pair of Jasper's pants and hardly looked at me. Daddy, on the other hand, looked at me long and hard.

"You sure about this?" he asked.

"I am, Daddy. Fact is I don't think I've ever been surer about anything in my whole life."

"Whole life, geeze," Mama said, "hardly call thirteen years a whole life."

Daddy took a step closer to me. "I'm still gonna keep my eye on you. If your schoolwork gets in trouble—"

"It won't, Daddy. You'll see."

I dropped my box near the door. "It's gonna be all right, Mama, I promise. I'll come visit nearly every day and you can come see me whenever you want. I'm just down the road, you know. Not like I'm moving to China. And I'll see you at church every Sunday."

Mama stuffed Jasper's pants between the arm of the chair and her thigh. She heaved a big sigh and then stood. "I'll see ya tomorrow, Luna." Then she smiled, a brave smile, but I could see the concern she had twitching at the corners of her mouth. "Give Luna a ride, Justus," she said. "Don't want the neighbors seeing her walking down the road carrying her belongings like that. They'll think she run away."

The twins and Jasper were on the porch. They didn't say much to me except good-bye. April hardly even looked my way, but June wrapped her arms around my legs. "Bye, Luna Fish."

Jasper folded his arms against his chest and took a stand on the steps. "Don't know why you wanna live there and not here."

I tousled his hair. He flinched. "You can come see me any time, and I'll come over all the time." Next I hugged Polly good and tight. She whimpered like she knew I was leaving. "I'll still be around, girl, don't you worry." She licked my face. "Keep an eye on Jasper—don't let him float away in the creek."

"Come on, Luna," Daddy said. "Let's get a move on."

I turned back and saw Mama standing at the screen. She raised her hand and made a tiny wave. I couldn't wave on account I was still holding the box in both arms. So I nodded and smiled. "I love you, Mama. This is gonna be fine."

"You can always change your mind, Luna. Ain't no rule against it."

CHAPTER
8

Ruby Day stood on the other side of the screen door and looked at me like she was staring down the barrel of a shotgun. Then she collected herself. "Luna, how come you came back? Forget somethin'?"

"No, Ruby Day, I come to stay with you. I'm going to take care of you now—forever. See, I got all my belongings in this box."

She backed off a step. "What? How come ... I mean ..." She stopped stammering and stared at me some more. "You can't do that, Luna. You got your own people."

"But you need help, and ... and besides, I promised Mason."

She pressed her nose against the screen. "Mason?"

"He made me promise a long time ago that if anything ever ... well you know, if it happened that I would care for you. So here I am." I swallowed. The lie got caught in my throat, but I forced it out. I'd ask God's forgiveness later on.

Ruby Day pushed open the screen, and I squeezed in past her. "It's gonna be fine, Ruby Day. We'll have a good time together." I dropped the box on the floor.

She flopped onto the sofa and shook a little. "You ask your mama and daddy 'bout this?"

"They said it was a fine idea."

Ruby Day made her way to the mantle and touched Mason's picture. "But ... but I ... I don't need no help. I'll be okay."

"No, Ruby Day, I want to help, and I already told you, I promised Mason."

"Ain't no truth in that and you know it, Luna. You just feelin' sorry for me. For the dumb retard down the block."

"Now, that ain't true. Even if I didn't actually promise Mason I'm ... I'm making the promise now." I snatched Mason's picture from her trembling hands. "I'm here now, Mason. And I promise to take care of your mama."

Ruby Day flopped on the couch again and held her head in her hands with her elbows resting on her knees. "I ... I wish I didn't need no help. Wish I weren't so ... feebleminded."

I sat next to her. "It's just the way God made you, and maybe you aren't like everybody else around here, but that doesn't make you stupid or well, like you're a mistake. But you do need help. And that's why I'm here."

Ruby Day swiped at tears and sniffled. "Okay, Luna."

Ruby Day's house only had two bedrooms, so I had to settle myself into Mason's room. Everything looked exactly the way it always did. A bed stood in the center of the room with a blue blanket on it. There was a tall dresser against the wall with Mason's record player on top. A small table near the head of the bed held a lamp that still had a shade painted with nursery rhymes on it. Ruby Day hadn't touched or moved a thing. I started to cry when I saw the stack of record albums on the floor.

I found some clean sheets in the hallway linen closet, and then I picked up dirty clothes off the floor. I opened a window and turned on the fan to let the musty boy smell out.

It wasn't hard to settle into a routine after that first day. I never realized how much I had learned from Mama about taking care of a house. Ruby Day went to work at the grocery store every morning like clockwork. She dressed, ate, and walked out the door at exactly the same time to catch the bus straight to Haskell's Grocery Store. It was almost like watching a ballet. And she returned every day at exactly 4:07 unless the bus was late. Whenever that happened it always made her nervous, and she'd walk in the front door all atwitter and apologetic like it was her fault that the bus driver had to help Mrs. Rooper coax her kitty cat, Mavis, out of the dogwood tree.

One time I went along with her in the morning. I wanted to see the exact route the bus took and to let Mr. Haskell know that I would be living with Ruby Day now.

"Morning, Ruby Day," said the bus driver.

"Morning, Cal," Ruby Day said.

I followed her to a seat about halfway down the aisle.

"There she is," I heard a woman say in a voice that wasn't quite low enough. "That dreadful retarded woman. You know, the one whose son got killed. It was a right shame, but I'm amazed they still let her work and all like she was a regular person."

I sat next to Ruby Day, but not before I managed to glare at the women.

"They shouldn't talk about you like that," I said.

Ruby Day looked out the window. "Ah, it don't bother me. Not so much anymore."

"But it still isn't nice. Women like that should know better."

The bus lurched and came to a stop at the next corner. The two women got up and walked past us. They stopped near the driver and dropped coins into the coin collector. One of the women looked back at us and Ruby Day smiled wide at her. "I hope you have a nice day."

I was surprised when the woman smiled back.

"It's like I always told Mason," Ruby Day said. "Being kind can make a mean person shine."

The bus stopped right out front of Haskell's Grocery Store. All in all it was about a ten-minute ride from home. Ruby Day dropped a token into the coin machine like it was a solemn event.

"You have a good day at work, Ruby Day," Cal said. "I'll be back to get you at four o'clock."

"Thank you," Ruby Day said.

Haskell's Grocery sat square in the middle of the block on Hill Street between Betty Lou's Beauty Parlor and Snipes Drug Store. I followed Ruby Day inside and watched her hang up her coat in a back room that smelled from a mixture of provolone cheese and coffee beans. She took a long card with her name on it from a rack on the wall near a funny-looking clock.

"This here is the time clock," she said. "I have to punch in every day and punch out every day. It's how Mr. Haskell keeps track of how many hours I worked."

Just then a woman wearing a white apron and hair piled on top of her head like a beehive walked into the room. "Ruby Day," she said. "Mr. Haskell needs you to clean up the mess in aisle three—four pickle jars busted."

"Okay, I'll do that, Lavinia," Ruby Day said.

Ruby Day and I walked to the pickle mess. It smelled pretty strong, but Ruby Day wasted no time cleaning the mess up and mopping the floor.

"No wonder you don't want to clean anything at home," I said.

Ruby Day laughed. "It's my job, Luna."

Then I saw Mr. Haskell strutting down the aisle. The look on his face told me he had something serious on his mind.

"Where's Lavinia?" he asked.

"Break room," Ruby Day said. "She told me to clean up the pickle jars."

He shook his head and twisted up his mouth. Then he said, "I told her to do it. Ruby Day, you get to the register when you finish and start bagging."

There was already a line six women deep at the register. Ruby Day introduced me to Flossie, a sweet-looking woman with curly brown hair and bright blue eyes.

"It's so nice to meet you," she said. "Will you be working here?"

Ruby Day laughed. "No, Flossie, Luna has school."

The next thing we saw was Lavinia running out of the break room.

"I wonder what happened," I said.

Mr. Haskell followed Lavinia. "I had to fire her. This was the last straw."

"Oh, I . . . I'm sorry," Ruby Day said. "I didn't mean to get Lavinia in trouble."

Mr. Haskell put his hand on Ruby Day's shoulder. "Not your fault."

"That's right," Flossie said. "You didn't do anything to get that woman canned."

There was a long enough pause in the conversation for me to jump in and tell Mr. Haskell what I came to tell him.

"Well, that's fine, Luna," he said. "I'm glad to know Ruby Day will be in good hands."

I stayed another couple of minutes. "I better get going, Ruby Day. I'll see you at home."

All in all I was glad I went to work with Ruby Day that morning. It helped me see how much people like Mr. Haskell cared about her and how some people treated her. It made me sort of upset to know that not everyone treated Ruby Day so nice.

I went to visit Mama most days and that was fine. I was there so much it was almost like I never left. Delores liked having extra drawers, at least according to April and June, but I hardly ever saw her. Delores was always running out to meet her friends.

"But I'm doing real good, Mama. Ruby Day is easy to be with most of the time, except when she gets to rattling so about subjects."

"Like what," Mama asked.

"Her flowers for one. And now that it's nearing the end of August, most of them are dying off and that makes her sad."

Mama and me sat on the porch during most of my visits, and as the days passed, it started to feel more and more like I was visiting and Mama started to have less patience with sitting on the porch. She'd say things like, "I got a lot of mending to do, Luna." Or, "It's 'bout time I peeled some potatoes for supper."

My little brother and sisters were getting ready to go back to school, but they hung around me like I was some visiting princess when I came by, and I will admit that I liked the feeling. Daddy, when I saw him—which wasn't too often—didn't seem to have much to say.

Life went on like that until the middle of September. Ruby Day worked each and every shift and spent the rest of her time watching TV or getting her garden ready for winter.

The worst part during that time was school. I started the eighth grade on schedule, but it was like walking into a foreign country. All the eyes in Mrs. Grady's class stared at me like I might have had squirrels on my head. One day that nasty Francine Whitaker even whispered to Wilma Burns. She didn't think I heard her, but I have good hearing. I heard her say, "Did you know Luna went to live with that feebleminded woman? That's what my mama calls her. They're like best friends now and that makes Luna feebleminded too. Only a moron would do what she's doin'."

I gave her such a glare that if it was a hand it would have knocked her off the chair. Not on account of her saying I was a retard, but on account of how she saw Ruby Day.

That afternoon I went to Mama and asked her about it. She was sitting on the porch with Polly as usual, shucking the last of the summer corn. "Luna," she said in that take-charge tone she had, "what do you think you should do about the girls at school?"

"I don't know. I can't keep people from talking, 'specially people who don't understand."

Mama kept right on shucking while I sat and thought about my problem. I scratched Polly behind the ears and every so often she whined or whimpered like she understood.

"You know," I said after a while. "Maybe I can help them understand."

"How so?"

"Maybe I can ask Mrs. Grady to let me talk to the

whole class and explain why I went to live with Ruby Day. You know? That might help."

Mama grew a grin as wide as an ear of corn. "That might work, Sweetheart. That might just work."

It was right after Mama said those words that I felt my back straighten. "Thank you, Mama, thank you. I'm going to do that tomorrow."

Mama shooed me off the porch with four ears of corn, instructions on how to boil it, and a kiss on the nose. "I am proud of you," she said.

CHAPTER
9

Ruby Day arrived home exactly on schedule that afternoon. She headed straight to her yard and started deadheading the roses. That was usually a signal that she had tough day. Mason told me once or twice that when Ruby Day felt angry or sad she would work in her garden until she felt better. I stood at the kitchen window and watched her. A whole half hour went by until I went outside. Gosh, it was warm that afternoon—even for mid-September.

"Ruby Day, are you okay?" I knelt down next to her.

"No, Luna. I am not okay today. Two girls laughed at me when I dropped a can of pork and beans on my toe."

"Pork and beans? Was it one them extra-big cans? Did you get hurt?"

She shook her head. "I don't know. I didn't look, because those girls made me cry, and I needed to hide my eyes."

"Is that all that happened?"

"Uhm huh, except ... except what Mr. Haskell said."

"What did Mr. Haskell say?" I patted her back.

She yanked at a clump of brown grass and tossed it over her shoulder. "He said he was giving me more money in my paycheck."

I smiled. "But that's a good thing, Ruby Day. You'll be making more money."

Ruby Day started to shake her head in that wild way she had. Then she balled her hands into fists and punched her head like she was trying to kill her thoughts inside.

"Stop that," I said with the same firmness my mama used with us kids. "Stop that this instant. There is nothing to be upset about." Then I stopped because I remembered how I hated it when Daddy would tell me I had no reason to be upset. I certainly did have a reason on most occasions.

"I'm sorry. Tell me why it upsets you to have more money."

"More to take care of, Luna. More to care about, and I don't like caring about those things."

I took her hands in mine and looked at her square in the face. "That's why I'm here. To be next to you and help you."

It took another minute or two, but Ruby Day settled down, and we went inside for corn and sliced ham.

The next morning I asked Mrs. Grady if I could talk to the class like I told Mama I wanted.

"Now why would you want to do such a thing?" She sat at her big oak desk and fiddled with pencils. "It's your business isn't it, Luna? Yours and your parents'."

"Well, that's just it. I had a talk with Mama yesterday while she was shucking corn, and that's when the notion struck me to stand up in front and tell everybody. I figured it could maybe keep people from whispering about me and Ruby Day."

Mrs. Grady shoved a pencil into her ratty nest of gray hair. "Go on, then. Say your piece, but don't take too much time. We have a full schedule today."

Mrs. Grady quieted everyone down, and I stood there with my back pressed against the blackboard. But my knees still knocked like two cymbals in a brass band. I thought for sure everyone could hear them.

"Now, class," Mrs. Grady said. "Luna Gleason has something to say."

I stared right at Francine, who was sitting all smug and tall. She wore a big red ribbon in her blonde hair that made me think of Christmas. I decided not to look at her as I spoke.

"I just wanted you all to know that I went to live with Ruby Day." Some snickers wafted around the room, but I ignored them. "Because she needs me more than I need to be living at home right now. Mason—" I swallowed. "Mason died, and now she's by herself, and Jesus said to help the widows and orphans, so that's what I intend to do."

Mrs. Grady stood up like she wanted me to sit down. But I stayed put and thought about my words some more.

"Sometimes a person has to follow Jesus—like the disciple fishermen."

I swallowed and tried to hide my sweaty palms. "That's all I got to say. Ruby Day needs me, and I would appreciate it if you all would stop calling her a retard or feebleminded. She didn't choose to be born that way. Not like Francine chose to wear that ... ostentatious bow this morning." I liked to use big words like *ostentatious* and *serendipity* from time to time. It makes people think or even get out the dictionary.

Some of the kids laughed, and I will admit I enjoyed the moment before I sat down. I made sure I gave Francine a look.

"Thank you, Luna," Mrs. Grady said. "Now please get out your geometry books and turn to page eighty-two. The isosceles triangle."

CHAPTER
10

Things got better after that. Ruby Day and I got into a routine, and I even started visiting Mama less. Somehow, Ruby Day managed to get Mr. Haskell to hire Lavinia back, and that made Lavinia start treating her better.

"She even made me a liverwurst sandwich for lunch the other day," Ruby Day said. "And she brought me a cream soda."

I was so proud of Ruby Day, and I knew Mason would be proud too.

About the second week of October, Ruby Day decided she should walk to the cemetery. I went with her. We brought flowers from the garden, and Ruby Day placed them gently on Mason's grave. We didn't stay very long—just long enough to say hello.

I still missed Mason, but the longer I stayed with Ruby Day, the more I felt the good parts of Mason were around me. I will confess that I was starting to feel a little tired from all the extra work, though. Now don't get me wrong, Mama and Daddy gave me chores, but when it came to cleaning up after Ruby Day — well, that was another story. She didn't seem to care where she let her clothes drop or give a lick to hanging wet towels up. I even had to teach her the proper way to scrub a pot.

Ruby Day was just fine with rinsing and drying, she just needed to learn how to fill the sink and soap up the dishes and pots and rinse them well. But we both agreed that drying was not always necessary.

Francine stopped bothering me at school, but Mrs. Grady kept giving me the stink eye. It was like she felt sorry for me or something. Every day it was the same question.

"How are you, Luna? How are you and Ruby Day getting along? Everything okay?"

I always said the same thing, "Yes, Ma'am, everything is fine." Then she'd say, "I'm glad to see you keeping your grades up."

And then I'd respond, "Yes, Ma'am. Daddy said he'd be watching on account of I still aim to go to college and become a teacher."

It wasn't the questions that bothered me as much as her tone. It was the same tone folks took with me right after Mason died. Mama called it "overblown concern," but she also said that most of the time people meant well, and I should just be glad people cared.

"Because, Luna," she said, "it's a rare thing in life to know someone cares about you—really cares, and not just because they have to."

One Saturday morning in late October there came a knock on the front door. Ruby Day was watching cartoons. She loved Bugs Bunny and the Roadrunner, and we enjoyed watching and laughing together as we ate bowls of cornflakes.

"Now who can that be?" I asked.

Ruby Day wasn't paying attention to me or anything else but the television, so I set my bowl on the coffee table and went to the door. A tall, skinny woman wearing what I think were two dead foxes around her shoulders stood on the other side. The foxes were sewn together tail-to-tail and had little beady glass eyes. The woman had short hair and wore a gray hat with a long feather sticking out of it, as well as pointy glasses and pointy shoes to match her pointy nose.

"Good morning," she said. She had the sound of a sophisticated lady from the city, like Mrs. Chalmers, the charm school woman, who came to school clear from Scranton to teach all the girls how to be polite in proper society and how to cross our legs at the ankles and the importance of proper posture.

She reached out her gloved hand. I didn't know if I should shake it or kiss it. I squeezed it lightly.

"My name is Sapphire Whitaker. I am looking for Ruby Day."

"Oh, Ruby Day. Yes, she's right in here, watching cartoons and ..."

The woman made a noise and pushed passed me.

"Ruby Day," Sapphire called.

I pushed past her and went to Ruby Day, who was by then standing up and staring at the sophisticated lady. A cornflake hung at the corner of Ruby Day's mouth.

"Just look at you," Sapphire said. She pulled a turquoise hanky from her purse and wiped Ruby Day's mouth. "I came as soon as I heard the news from Uncle Charles. He heard it from a Fuller Brush man who comes to this ... this town now and again."

I watched Ruby Day swallow. She balled her hands into tight fists like she was going to start pounding on something, but just as she brought them up to her temples she stopped. Like she had thought better of it.

"Ruby Day, do you know her?"

She nodded and tried to speak, but the woman spoke for her. "I am Ruby Day's Aunt Sapphire from Philadelphia. Bryn Mawr, actually." She pulled off her gloves and handed them to me. Then she turned around and let her foxes slip from her shoulders. I had no choice but to catch them like I was the maid or a fur trapper or something. I tossed the articles on a chair, and I think Sapphire would have exploded if Ruby Day hadn't found her voice in time.

"How come you came here?" Ruby Day said. "I never told you to come."

"Oh dear, where are your manners? Aren't you going to invite me to sit?"

Ruby Day flopped down. Sapphire chose the overstuffed armchair. She grimaced when her hands touched the fabric.

"May I get you a drink?" I asked, not wanting to be pegged for not having any class.

"That would be fine, dear."

"I can make coffee."

"I'm certain you can."

I headed for the kitchen wondering if I had just been complimented or insulted. And I didn't know if I should make coffee or get a glass of water. The truth was I smelled a rat. A dirty, stinking, high-society rat, and I wanted to get to the kitchen to call Mama.

After I got coffee percolating, I set out three cups and saucers on a tray. I looked at the telephone on the wall and thought about calling Mama. I dialed home. One ring, two, three, but I hung up quickly. I had told Mama I could handle it and that meant everything — even Aunt Sapphire.

I returned to the living room and stood next to Ruby Day. "My name is Luna Gleason," I said. "I've been helping out Ruby Day since the funeral and all."

"How nice," Sapphire said. "Fortunately you won't be needing to ... to help any longer. I've come to take Ruby Day home."

Now I really wished Mama was home, and I sailed a silent wish that she would get one of her worry thoughts and come banging on the front door.

"Home?" I said. "But Ruby Day is home. Right here. In this house."

I watched Ruby Day's bottom lip start to quiver, and I worried that she'd throw off her glasses and start that shrieking thing she did. But instead I only saw three tears roll down her cheek. Sapphire wiped them with her high-society hanky.

"There, there, Ruby Day. It's for the best."

Ruby Day grabbed my hand and pulled me down onto the sofa next to her.

"I ain't goin', Aunt Sapphire. I got Luna here to help me and I got a job and—"

Sapphire clicked her mouth like it was a chicken beak. That was it. She looked like an overgrown chicken. I suppressed a smile. "Now, now, Ruby Day. That's just it. Now that Mason is ... well, no longer with us ... there's no reason for you to work and ... keep this bright young woman with you. I'm sure she's got future plans. Don't you, dear?"

I nodded my head something fierce. "Yes, Ma'am, I'm planning on going to college and becoming a teacher. But that don't mean I can't still live here with Ruby Day. We're fine—honest we are."

That was when the doorbell rang, and I hoped with all my heart it was Mama.

Nope, just the paperboy. "Whose fancy car is that?" he asked.

"Just a visitor, Tom." I reached into a cleaned-out peanut butter jar on the mantel that we dropped coins in every now and again and paid Tom a nickel for the paper.

"Thank you, Luna." He craned his neck trying to get a good look into the living room, but I shooed him out the door. Rumors had a way of firestorming through Makeshift County, and I figured by the end of the day there'd be a story floating around about some visiting princess from a faraway land who drove a fancy car and wore dead foxes on her shoulders.

I got back to the sofa in time to hear Sapphire say, "Now you don't have to leave today. Take two or three days, if you like, to pack and say your good-byes. I'll be back Tuesday to take you home."

"Where you going?" Ruby Day asked.

"Back to Bryn Mawr, of course. I'd return sooner but I have a ... well, a thing at the Cricket Club."

"Cricket Club," I said. "You mean real crickets? The kind that chirp when they rub their legs together?"

Aunt Sapphire laughed like a fat man. "No, no, you dear child. The Cricket Club is ... well a country club for—"

Obviously the humor was lost on Aunt Sapphire. "I get it. High society folk and all. You mean it's a club for snobs." I wanted to push the words back inside my mouth, but I didn't. I really didn't mean it to be sassy.

"We are not snobs, young lady. But you are correct about one thing. We are not ... ordinary."

She clicked her beak and turned her face away with a huff, and I figured I had just pretty much sealed the deal with Aunt Sapphire. There was no way now I was going to get her to like me.

And that was that. Sapphire stood and indicated to me to help her with her dead foxes. Once I did she sashayed out of the house, down the walk, and into her fancy car. I saw a man with a funny hat sitting behind the wheel.

"Look at him," I said. "He must be one of them chauffeurs. Imagine having someone drive you all over the place like that. Why, Daddy would have a conniption fit if anyone tried to drive for him."

Ruby Day stood in the cold air on the porch hugging herself and crying.

"Come on inside, Ruby Day. It's too cold out here. And why are you crying?"

She shook her head and kept on shaking like a dog after a good soaking. I tried to pull her inside, but

Ruby Day could get mighty strong. It was like she had glued herself to that spot, and there she stood for a good fifteen or more minutes shaking and crying and shivering.

The coming of Aunt Sapphire was not good news.

CHAPTER

11

One of the things I learned from Mason was that when Ruby Day got into one of her stubborn jags, it was best to let her be until she worked it out. Mason told me that sometimes she would stand on the porch or in the kitchen or in her garden for more than an hour crying and shaking. I sincerely hoped that this was not one of those occasions.

I sat down on the porch swing and rocked slowly back and forth, back and forth, and that brought back a flood of memories that I wished I didn't have. Mason and I used to sit on the swing and listen to his jazz records. He would turn it up loud inside the house so we could hear it on the porch.

"Now this," he said one night, "is Charlie Parker."

He called him a genius on the saxophone. I liked

Charlie Parker well enough. I liked the way the music would jiggle and bebop through the air and tickle my ears. But mostly I liked sitting with Mason. He told me all sorts of things about jazz and music. But never in all the time I knew him did Mason mention Aunt Sapphire.

It was nearly lunchtime before Ruby Day finally sobbed herself dry and went into the house. She plunked down on the sofa, exhausted. She took Mason's picture from the side table and hugged it to her chest.

"I won't be going," she said. "I won't be leaving Mason, and I won't be leaving you, Luna. You're like my daughter now." It was the clearest I ever heard her explain what was sitting so heavy on her heart.

I sat next to her and patted her knee. She wore a flowery housedress on account of it was Saturday, and that was what she wore every Saturday to watch cartoons.

"Why, Ruby Day, that's the nicest thing anyone ever said about me. I like having two mamas."

She set the picture back on the table and then gave me a bear hug that nearly popped the stuffing out of me. But Ruby Day was like that. Sometimes she didn't know her own strength.

She tugged on a stray thread in the hem of her dress and twirled it around her index finger until it turned the color of an overripe plum. "I'm supposed to be out of my dress by now and in my garden clothes."

"I know, Ruby Day. You can still get changed and work in the garden."

"Don't want to, Luna."

I turned off the television and sat back down. It was obvious that she had some explaining to do about Aunt Sapphire. But expecting Ruby Day to explain anything was a little like listening to Pastor Davis explain the Trinity. It just left you with more questions. But I had to start somewhere. Aunt Sapphire apparently had some kind of say in Ruby Day's life, and I needed to get to the bottom of it.

Sapphire seemed a powerful woman with powerful opinions. Still, I couldn't figure how a person could blow into town, make demands, blow out again, and expect someone like Ruby Day to follow along.

"Ruby Day, how come you never told me about Aunt Sapphire and Bryn Mawr and all?"

"Didn't need to, Luna. Long as I had Mason, didn't need to." She untwirled the string from her finger. "Sapphire said as long as Mason could help me it would be all right to stay."

"Then why does she want you to go back there? You're doing fine right here. And I'm here."

Ruby Day swiped at her tears and ran her palm over the top of Mason's picture. "Don't know. Sapphire is just like that. She's so rich and all."

"But rich doesn't give her any special rights to tell you where to live. She might look like a queen in all her fancy getup and hat and pointy glasses, but she doesn't have any right to tell you where to live. Ain't no rule about it."

Ruby Day pulled her glasses off. She cleaned them with her dress. "Sapphire sent me here ... with Mason."

"To Makeshift?"

Ruby Day nodded her head so hard I thought it might fling right off her shoulders.

"How come?" Other than right after Mason's funeral, I'd never thought much about Ruby Day not living in Makeshift. I mean, she was always just there and Mason was always my friend. I never remembered them moving into town. Their arrival was a mystery, and now all of a sudden I needed to solve it. Especially if Sapphire was involved.

"After my daddy died. She said I embarrassed her, so she sent us here. To this house."

Ruby Day went quiet, and I stared at Mason's picture, wishing he could give me more answers.

"Luna," Ruby Day said. "I think I want to change into my garden clothes."

I nodded. "You go ahead. We'll figure this out later."

Ruby Day started up the stairs, stopped, and said, "I ain't going back with Aunt Sapphire."

"I know. I heard you say that. Don't worry."

My stomach growled. I figured if I was hungry then so was Ruby Day, so I went into the kitchen. I opened two cans of tomato soup and plopped the contents into a pot with two cans of milk. I stirred and stirred and watched the mixture turn dusty rose. Next I made two grilled cheese sandwiches just like Mama taught me, with butter inside and out.

I thought about calling Mama and telling her what happened, but I really didn't know what *had* happened. It seemed simple enough to me that if Ruby Day wanted to stay in Makeshift, she should. How could even a force so seemingly powerful as Sapphire make that happen if she didn't want it?

Ruby Day walked into the kitchen carrying a shoebox closed tight with gobs of masking tape. She was wearing her garden clothes—blue jeans with rolled-up cuffs and a flannel shirt.

"Whatcha got there?" I asked.

"Papers. Stuff Sapphire told me to keep."

"Certainly has a lot of tape."

"Mason did it when he was little. I kept dropping it and things poured out on the floor."

I turned the sandwiches over and pressed them down as flat as I could with my spatula. They sizzled as the buttery and cheesy aroma rose to the ceiling. "Sit down. I made lunch."

"Not hungry," Ruby Day said.

"Doesn't matter. You have to eat, especially if we're going to fight Aunt Sapphire."

Ruby Day plopped onto a kitchen chair. "Fight? I don't want to fight her."

"I don't mean with our fists. I mean we're going to fight to keep you here. In Makeshift. She can't force you to go. You're an adult, Ruby Day."

She started to cry again. "No . . . I'm not, Luna. My brain is not. Sapphire said so. Everybody said so. Even Mason said so."

I used the spatula to cut her sandwich into four triangles and then arranged them on a large blue dish around a bowl of tomato soup.

"It looks good, Luna. You make good soup. Just like Mason."

I triangled my sandwich and joined her at the table, but just like Ruby Day, I had yet to taste my food. I couldn't stop looking at the shoebox. But I knew I couldn't take it away and open it without her permission. She could easily fly into one her fits. It had to be her idea.

"Are you going to show me what's in the box?"

Ruby Day shook her head and slammed her palm onto the lid. "Can't, Luna. I changed my mind."

Ruby Day and I talked about Aunt Sapphire for a little longer while we ate. It turned out that Ruby Day's family had money—lots of it.

She said they made money in textiles. I had to look that up because Ruby Day said she knew the word, not what it meant.

"Then how come you never got any of the money?" I asked.

"Because it was put away." She patted the box. "Sapphire put my money away for the rest of my life."

"It's in the shoebox? Aunt Sapphire put all your money in the shoebox?"

Ruby Day laughed so hard she snorted tomato soup out her nose. "Noooooo. Uncle Charles took the money."

"Uncle Charles?" I wanted to ask more questions but Ruby Day's hands shook as she ate her soup. She took a deep, shaky breath and let it out through her nose. I watched her ball her little hands into fists, and I grabbed them both before she could start hitting herself.

"You don't need to do that. I promise I will get this ironed out—somehow. But you might need to show me what's in the box."

She snatched it off the table quicker than a mouse-trap. "No. I can't do it right now, Luna Gleason. I can't do it."

CHAPTER
12

A bad thunderstorm blew into town that night, the same way Aunt Sapphire blew into our lives—out of nowhere. Ruby Day didn't like storms, and I expected her to come into my room to wait it out with me. But she never showed up, even though the wind whipped around the little house and made the shutters bang against the clapboard. It was scary even for me. Every so often, lightning split the sky and lit up my room for just an instant, but still long enough to see the pictures on the walls.

Mason's walls were covered with pictures of his favorite jazz musicians cut out from magazines, and, well, to be honest, their faces flashing on and off all night was a little bit creepy. Thunder rolled so close overhead I could almost feel the weight of it.

I think I even missed Delores that night, Delores and the twins. Loud, nasty thunderstorms were definitely easier to get through with sisters around.

The next morning I found Ruby Day asleep in the living room on the floor. She had curled up on the rug near the hearth. The shoebox was next to her, and a slew of pictures were spread out all around her on the floor. A large ball of wadded-up masking tape had been tossed into the fireplace. Her glasses were in the shoebox, and I had the impression she ripped them off her face and tossed them in there because something made her angry.

"Ruby Day." I shook her shoulder slightly. "Wake up now, Ruby Day."

She stirred and looked around. I placed her glasses on her face. "Ruby Day. You're in the living room. You fell asleep out here. How you slept through that storm, I'll never know."

But from the looks of the photographs strewn around, I figured she had her own storm to get through.

She rallied a bit more and sat up on the couch. "I'm . . . I'm sorry, Luna. I was looking."

"Looking for what?" I sat next to her. "Is there something you need to tell me?"

She reached down and snagged a photo from the floor. "This is a picture of me—back . . . there."

I held the black-and-white image of a young woman standing outside a large house. It had columns and long windows, a wide wraparound porch, and a lawn that must have been ten sizes bigger than Mama and Daddy's.

"Is this you?"

Ruby Day nodded. "Before Mason."

"You look so pretty. Where is this house? Is it Aunt Sapphire's house in Bryn Mawr?"

Ruby Day shook her head violently again. She balled up her fists and smacked her temples. I grabbed her hands and pulled them down to her lap. "Ruby Day. Ruby Day, what's wrong?"

"Don't want to go back, Luna."

"What is this place, Ruby Day? Where was this picture taken?"

She rubbed her eyes under her glasses and snuffed back tears and snot.

"Don't want to go back."

"I know, I know. You won't have to. I promise," I said, even though I didn't know why she was so scared. Or why she was showing me the picture now. I took the opportunity to look at the other pictures without touching them. There were mostly photos of people standing around in small groups, near that same large house.

Ruby Day picked up another picture. "This is my daddy. He's dead. Like Mason."

I looked into the eyes of a man with perfectly round glasses, a balding head, a large nose, and the kindest smile I had ever seen in my life. "He looks nice."

Ruby Day sat back on her heels and rocked. She whimpered with a sound like a little cat. My heart raced on account of I didn't know what to do. I let Ruby Day rock and whimper for another minute or two until I said, "Ruby Day, I think you should go in your room and rest. You couldn't have gotten a good night's sleep on this hard floor."

Ruby Day stopped rocking. "Okay, I'll go."

I helped her up and led her toward the steps. "Go on," I said. "Get under your covers and sleep. I'll clean up the mess."

For a second I thought I saw something like fear flash in Ruby Day's eyes as she looked over at the spilled contents of the shoebox. But then she yawned. "It's gonna be okay, right Luna?"

What else could I say? "I know it will. Isn't that God's promise—all things work together for what's best."

I watched Ruby Day climb the stairs. *Sometimes God's best isn't always what we want*, I thought.

The contents of Ruby Day's shoebox were scattered everywhere. Considering how secretive she was about it, I was surprised she didn't insist on cleaning it up before going to bed, but then again, Ruby Day didn't always remember to make the wisest choice. I rifled through the pictures hoping to see something that would clue me in on why Sapphire wanted Ruby Day to move back to Philadelphia.

I saw another photo on the floor and grabbed it. It was also Ruby Day standing in front of the same house, but there was a small sign in that photo that read *Henry R. Mason Home for the Feebleminded.*

Home for the Feebleminded? I had heard of places like that from Mama. She said that Ruby Day was fortunate she had never been sent to such a home. But now it appeared that the real truth about Ruby Day was coming out. And Aunt Sapphire was in on it.

I called Mama.

"Mama," I said. "I got to talk to you and Daddy."

"Is something wrong? Is Ruby Day all right?"

"Oh, Mama. Something is wrong and Ruby Day is not all right."

"Do you want me to come over there, Luna?" Mama's voice sounded sweet and comforting. Just like always. "Is she hurt or sick?"

"No. She's not hurt or sick. Can you come in a little while? Will Daddy skip church this morning? I don't think I should bring Ruby Day to church."

"I don't know, Luna. You know how he is, and today is Communion Sunday."

"But Mama, this is really important."

"I'll talk to him."

I hung up the phone and went to check on Ruby Day. She was sound asleep under her baby blue quilt. From where I stood in the doorway, looking at her, you couldn't really tell that Ruby Day was retarded or feebleminded or any of the other words they've come up with to describe her.

I needed to take a deep breath, which I did, and then I let it out slowly like Mama told me to do when I felt worried.

"Don't you fret, Ruby Day," I whispered as I closed the door. "I'll figure something out. I promised Mason I'd take care of you, and that's what I'm gonna do."

CHAPTER
13

I hurried to gather all the photos back into Ruby Day's shoebox—all except the two pictures of her near that horrible sign.

Just as I set the box on the dining room table, I recognized Mama's voice on the porch.

"It won't matter that we miss church," I heard her say through the opened window. "Luna needs us. Ain't no rule that a body has to be in church every single Sunday. Helping people who need it can be just as much worship as sitting in a pew singing hymns."

"Well, that might be true, but Luna should be in church too. Probably nothing we can't handle after," I heard Daddy say.

I waited to open the door until Mama knocked, just so they wouldn't think I was standing there listening to them.

"Mama." I gave her a big hug and held on for an extra second or two. Next I hugged Daddy, but not for as long a time.

"What's going on, Luna Fish?" Mama asked.

"It's about Ruby Day."

"Figured as much," Daddy said. "I knew there'd be trouble."

We all went to the living room.

"Where is she?" Mama asked.

"I made her go to bed. She slept on the floor all night."

Mama sat on the sofa. Daddy stood with his hands in his pockets. "What do you mean she slept on the floor?" Daddy said.

"She has a shoebox filled with pictures and she was looking at them all last night. I found her asleep this morning."

"What pictures?" Mama asked.

"Like this." I held the picture of Ruby Day out to her. She took it and studied it a second. "Home for the Feebleminded? Is that Ruby Day? Wow, she looks so young."

"Yes, Mama, that's Ruby Day. And the picture made her awful upset. Do you think it could be why she's so afraid of Aunt Sapphire?"

"Aunt Sapphire?" Mama said. "Who in the world is she?"

"She's a woman who showed up here yesterday

and started saying that Ruby Day had to go back to Philadelphia with her—now that Mason is . . . is gone. But I don't believe her." I looked at my daddy. "Do you think Ruby Day is afraid she'll have to go back to this . . . feebleminded home?" I looked at Mama. "If you met Sapphire, you'd know. She has dead foxes and a snooty face. We can't let that happen. You told me they're terrible places. They treat people so mean."

"Aunt Sapphire?" Daddy said. "You saying this is a family matter? We are not getting stuck in family matters. Family is family, and even though you live here, Luna, you are not Ruby Day's family."

That was when Ruby Day nearly stumbled down the steps. She pounded her temples in time with her steps. "Is so. Luna is like my own daughter. She takes care of me—like Mason did, only he was a boy. Luna is a girl."

"I know. I know," Mama said. "Let's just settle down and see what we can figure out." Mama looked at me. "Luna, make some tea for me and Ruby Day. Now, Ruby Day, you come on over here and sit."

"Okay, Mama." I looked at Daddy, who decided to sit in the big chair. He was wearing his Sunday suit with his shiny shoes and white socks sticking up. "You want anything, Daddy?"

"No. I just want to get on with it." He checked his watch.

I put the kettle on to boil and waited. I knew Mama

well. I knew she would want to sit with Ruby Day with no words for a minute or two. It was her way. She always said that there wasn't any rule that said people had to be talking all the time. Sometimes just sitting quietly was required. I peeked into the living room and knew without a doubt that Mama was correct in her estimation that day. Ruby Day had her head on Mama's shoulder while Mama gently stroked her hair.

Mama looked so pretty. But she always did. Her Sunday dress was mostly beige but had tiny green vines all over it. And she wore a little hat with a beige veil that barely covered her eyebrows. I was still in my pajamas.

I prepared the tea the way everyone liked it. Mama drank hers with milk. Ruby Day liked milk and sugar. I even made a cup for Daddy, without anything in it, just in case he changed his mind, and carried the heavy tray into the living room.

"Now tell me, Luna. What in the world happened?"

"Like I said, Mama. Aunt Sapphire happened." I sat in the rocking chair.

"Family matters," Daddy said. "I don't want to get involved in family matters."

Ruby Day started to talk but Mama hushed her. "Ruby Day, you just stay calm and drink your tea. Let Luna tell the story."

I sipped my tea and started to tell them what happened.

"And then I showed you that picture," I said in the end.

Mama took the picture, and for a minute it looked like she was praying over it. Then she looked into Ruby Day's frightened eyes. "Is this where you lived, Ruby Day?"

Ruby Day nodded and smashed her glasses into her face.

"And this is where you think Aunt Sapphire wants you to go?"

Ruby Day nodded.

"Oh, Mama," I said. "We can't let it happen."

Daddy snatched the picture from Mama's hand. "Louise, I'm telling you, family is family. Can't mess in family business."

"Now, Justus," Mama said, "this ain't right on any account. I heard about these places." She removed her hat and set it on the coffee table. "Dreadful. Just dreadful."

"What can we do?" Daddy said. "We can't keep Ruby Day here if her family has other plans. They probably know what's best for her."

"But Daddy, you said I couldn't carry Mason and I did. I did that just fine. You said I'd never bait a proper hook, and I do that like a champ because Mason taught me. Ain't you the one who is always saying, 'I can do all things through Christ who strengtheneth me'? All things, Daddy, not just some things. Even fight Aunt Sapphire and her fancy foxes and big car."

"But some things are not ours to fight," Daddy said.

I swallowed and looked at Mama. "I have to try."

Mama patted Ruby Day's knee. "When is Sapphire coming back? Do you know?"

"Tuesday. She said Tuesday."

Mama stood. "Okay. There is not much we can do today." She pinned her hat back in place. "Come along, Justus. We can still make Communion."

"Will you come back after church?"

Mama touched my cheek and then kissed me. "How 'bout if you and Ruby Day come for Sunday supper? I'm making chicken and dumplings."

"Okay, Mama."

There were only a couple of things in life more inviting than Mama's chicken and dumplings—Christmas and a good book.

I walked them to the door.

"See you at two," Mama said. "And don't worry too much about Ruby Day. Just go about the day as usual. Let her work in the garden or read her a story. She likes that."

Daddy put his hand on my shoulder. "You might not win this battle, Luna."

"But I'm gonna fight it, Daddy."

CHAPTER
14

After Mama and Daddy left, Ruby Day hardly said a word, just tinkered in her garden and in her room until it was time to leave for Mama's house.

She'd left the shoebox on the dining room table. I passed by it three or four times until I finally decided to take another look through the contents. There had to be something inside that would explain why Aunt Sapphire was so bent on taking Ruby Day back.

I made sure Ruby Day was still in the backyard before I opened the box. Nothing jumped out at first. Not until I dropped the lid. When I picked it up I found a white envelope with something scribbled on the front in black ink taped to the underside. I only recognized the first letter, *D*. But before I could open it, Ruby Day wandered into the dining room.

"Whatcha doing, Luna? Looking for more pictures?"

I held the envelope behind my back. "N-n-no, Ruby Day. I was just cleaning up. I guess we should be getting to Mama's now."

"Okay, Luna. I'll go change back into my Sunday dress. Will you help me zip up the back?"

I folded the white envelope in half and shoved it into my jeans' pocket. It would have to wait. Probably nothing important anyway.

Ruby Day and I left for Mama's just a few minutes later. Ruby Day was a quick dresser, and I didn't bother to change out of the clothes I was wearing. I helped Ruby Day button up her peacoat, and I buttoned mine. I managed to slip the envelope into my coat pocket without Ruby Day seeing me.

The day was bright but cold, with not a single cloud in the sky—unusual for October. The storm left a bright, clear day behind, with a sky so blue it seemed painted on—like a watercolor—and the air carried that nutty, brown smell of autumn. The sun felt good on my shoulders as we walked down the street. I thought about asking Ruby Day about the envelope, but before I could the twins jumped out from behind some bushes. "You coming home, Luna?" they said.

We stopped fast. Ruby Day almost tripped over her feet, and I drew her arm close to mine. "Don't do that, you two," I said. "You startled Ruby Day—and me."

"Ah, we're sorry," said April. "But how 'bout it, Luna? You coming home?"

"For Sunday supper," Ruby Day said.

"Mama's making chicken and dumplings," said June. Then she grabbed April's hand and they ran off toward the house. I smiled because I guess I kind of missed them—in a way.

Delores sat on the front porch steps. She wore a blue skirt with a white sweater and white knee-high socks and brown and white saddle shoes from Buster Brown. She looked like she was waiting for someone. Probably Carl Yeager.

"Well, look what the cat dragged in," Delores said.

"Hey, Delores. Waiting for a bus?" I said.

"I've been invited to Carl's for Sunday supper. Daddy said I could go on account of you and Ru—" She looked at Ruby Day and smiled with that fake smile of hers. "Afternoon, Ruby Day."

"Afternoon, Delores. You look so pretty."

Delores straightened her back. "Why thank you, Ruby Day. And you look very pretty too."

I knew she didn't mean it.

"Anyhoo," Delores said, "Daddy told me I could go to Carl's house on account of you and Ruby Day coming, and that way there'd be more room at the table, but I think they just don't want me there."

"How come you think that?" I asked.

"I heard Mama and Daddy talking about you and

Ruby Day and someone named Sapphire—what a crazy name. I don't think any of you want me there."

I smiled and tightened my grip on Ruby Day's hand. "Don't take it too personal, Delores, but you know how you can be."

"What? How can I be?"

"Let's just say you don't have any trouble saying what's on your mind, and sometimes that can be—"

"All right, all right. I get it. Have a nice supper." She said the last part in her snooty voice. Then she moved a little to the left and let us past her up the steps.

"Have a good time," I said.

"Oh, I will. I always have a good time with Carl. He's . . . dreamy."

I shook my head and felt my eyes roll in their sockets.

I pushed open the door and breathed deep. There was nothing like the aroma of Mama's cooking—no matter what she was making. I think my Mama was the best cook in Makeshift County and maybe even all of Pennsylvania. The other mothers were always coming to Mama and asking her opinion on recipes or for directions on how to pluck a pheasant or make a meatloaf or mashed potatoes. Sometimes I thought she should have gone to some fancy cooking school like they had in Paris and become a famous chef.

Sometimes when I went to the library, or the Bookmobile came into town, I checked out cookbooks for Mama so she could try out new recipes. Once she made something she called crepes with strawberries and whipped cream. I didn't think there was any recipe Mama couldn't make.

When we reached the kitchen, I heard her singing "How Great Thou Art." Mama had a nice voice too.

"I like to hear singing," Ruby Day said. "It makes my heart glad."

Polly Dog came bounding down the steps with her tail wagging a mile a minute. I crouched down and hugged her with all my might. "I miss you too, girl." She licked my cheek.

Mama walked into the living room drying her hands on her apron. She chose her autumn apron decorated with pumpkins and green vines and squash, which matched her Sunday dress.

"Luna, Ruby Day," she said. "Supper will be ready in just a minute or two. Sit and rest a bit."

"Where's Daddy?" I asked. "Taking his nap?"

"Yes," Mama said. "Nothing's really changed around here. Daddy is still Daddy. He'll be down in plenty of time."

She was right about that. Daddy had an uncanny knack for waking from his Sunday nap and walking into the dining room at the precise moment Mama put the main course—a roast or a stew or whatever it was—on the hot plate on the dining room table.

Mama went back to the kitchen and to her singing, so

Ruby Day and I sat on the couch. It was old and smelled a little bit from years of spills and animals lounging on it. But it was comfortable and just plain good to sit on again. It felt so nice to be in my old house. I loved our living room, and I will confess that I missed its spaciousness sometimes. Ruby Day's house was a postage stamp in comparison. But Mama always said with six children and a dog running around, she needed a big house. Thinking about it though, I was glad I only had to clean Ruby Day's place.

Jasper came bounding down the stairs. "Luna," he called. And then he tackled me. "You come for Sunday supper?"

"Yep. How ya doin', Jasper?"

He settled himself down and looked at Ruby Day. "She staying too?"

"Yes," I said.

"Okay," Jasper said. "Luna, I found a turtle down at the creek. Mama let me keep him in a bucket out back, but just for a while. Then I had to let him go."

"That's nice."

The front door swung open. "Mama," Delores called. "I'm leaving." She didn't wait for an answer, but then again, she never did.

Mama came into the living room. "Was that Delores?"

"Yes, Mama, I guess Carl came by and got her in that old jalopy of his. I don't like him."

"Now, now, Luna. Let's not judge. He's a nice boy."

"Must be. He puts up with Delores," I said.

Ruby Day giggled like I hadn't heard her giggle since before Sapphire blew into town. It was good to hear.

"Now that's more like it," Mama said. "Supper is ready. Would you call the twins, Luna? You can come with me, Ruby Day."

Mama took Ruby Day's hand and led her into the dining room. I stepped out onto the porch and called for April and June at the top of my lungs. They were probably swinging from some tree branches down the road.

But Sunday supper was not something anyone wanted to miss, and they came running quicker than bugs on roses. April had something in her hands. "Look what I found, Luna. Look."

It was an itty-bitty garter snake.

"You put that down, April."

"No, I wanna show Mama. I caught him all by myself."

April dashed through the front door, and I followed. Polly barked like crazy at her and the snake and tried to corral April near the front door. But April pushed her aside. "Look, Mama. A snake!"

"A snake," called Mama. "You toss that thing outside this *instant*."

"Oh, cool," hollered Jasper. "Let me see him."

"Come on, you two," I said. "Let the snake go. Poor thing. You're gonna kill it."

Polly barked and jumped, trying to get the snake.

"Go on, now. Mama said to toss it outside."

"Aw, gee," April said. "I want to keep him. Mama let Jasper keep the turtle."

Ruby Day walked in, and she leaned over to peek at the snake. "Mason used to catch snakes sometimes. That one's kind of cute." April beamed up at Ruby Day, and Ruby smiled back.

That was when Mama came back to the living room. "Well, I don't think it's cute, and I won't keep a snake. Now do as I say if you want any supper."

April stamped her foot and took the snake outside.

After the snake was disposed of, I sat next to Ruby Day, who was sitting in Delores's usual spot. Everyone else took their usual seats. As if on cue, Daddy walked into the room the exact moment Mama set the steaming crock of chicken and dumplings on the table.

Daddy sat at the head of the table, closest to the stew.

"Looks good, Louise," Daddy said. Then we all joined hands.

"Heavenly Father," Daddy said. "We thank thee for this food and for thy goodness. We thank thee for our guest, Ruby Day, and for Luna, who came to eat with us this fine Sunday afternoon. We ask that you bless this food to our bodies, and our bodies to thy service. In Jesus' name, amen."

Then we dropped hands and started serving food. The children chitter-chattered and Mama passed rolls and butter and a bowl of peas around.

Ruby Day filled her plate with stew and peas and ate like tomorrow wasn't coming. It did my heart good to see her enjoy Mama's cooking. I enjoyed it as well. Mama made the best dumplings. I loved to watch her make them. She'd mix the flour and milk and salt and then drop the dumplings one by one onto the bubbling stew. The blobs always sank to the bottom like small, white rocks, but then something magical happened, and they turned light and fluffy and rose to the top. That's how you knew they were done. Light and airy, Mama called them. Daddy called them delicious, and always smiled when he ate them.

"So, how come Ruby Day is eatin' with us?" Jasper asked.

"She was invited," Mama said. "Now finish up and then you all go outside to play. Luna and Ruby Day and Daddy and me got some discussing to do."

"Is Luna moving back?" April asked.

"No," I said. "I'm still living at Ruby Day's, and I think I always will."

Daddy swallowed hard. "Well, until you go to college."

I looked at him and watched his tattoo ripple. "I think I should go to a college around here, Daddy. That way I can still live with Ruby Day."

He glared at me. Mama touched his arm. "Not now, Justus. Eat your meal."

Daddy pointed his fork at me. "We'll talk about this, Luna Fish."

Ruby Day dropped her fork and started to cry.

"Now see what you did, Daddy," I said.

Ruby Day shook her head. "It ain't that, Luna. You can go to college. Mason was all set to go but ..." Her voice trailed off into a whisper.

Mama clapped her hands. "Okay. Children. Out the door."

"But I ain't done," Jasper said.

"Dessert on the porch," Mama said.

"Oh, boy," said April and June. "Dessert on the porch." They held hands and skipped outside. Jasper followed quickly behind, chewing on a chunk of chicken.

I wiped my mouth with my napkin—Mama always used her best cloth napkins on Sunday. Today's were brown with white eyelet edging. It made me wonder what kind of napkins Aunt Sapphire used. She probably had a servant to wipe her mouth for her. The thought made me wince at first, and then I thought of someone wiping her face like she was a baby.

And then I thought about the envelope in my coat pocket.

Mama cleared some of the plates. When she started getting close to Daddy, he said, "I'd like to finish my meal." He gave Mama a quick half smile. "Ruby Day's problem will still be a problem five minutes from now."

"Don't make your husband go fast," Ruby Day said. "I'm sorry I got everybody so ... so out of kilter. It's just Sapphire. She gets me sorta riled sometimes. Always did."

"Don't you fret, honey," Mama said. She put her hand on Ruby Day's shoulder. "I'll go bring the children their pudding while Justus finishes his meal." Then she looked at Daddy. "I wasn't going to take your plate, dear. I know how you like your chicken and dumplings."

Daddy winked. "I sure do, Louise."

Mama kissed his cheek, and my heart gladdened on account I thought it was nice that Mama and Daddy loved each other so much that even dumplings could make them smile.

When supper ended and the dishes were cleared, Mama said we could wait on washing until after we talked more about Ruby Day's problem.

Daddy sat in his chair, Mama in her rocker, and Ruby Day and I sat next to each other on the blue sofa. Jasper ran back inside, but not for long. Mama shooed him out quicker than a fly in summer. "Go on, boy," she said. "This ain't none of your beeswax."

We were all quiet a minute or two until Daddy started. "Now what is the trouble? Will someone please explain to me why Ruby Day is so all-fired upset? And what does Aunt Emerald—"

"Sapphire," I said. "I only know she's fixing to take Ruby Day back to Philadelphia and put her back in the home for the feebleminded. Ruby Day believes it too."

Daddy's eyes grew wide. "Feebleminded? Ruby Day is not feebleminded. I hate that word. She's just a little slower on the draw than some of us—not most, but some."

Ruby Day smiled.

"But that's what she's fixin' to do," I said. "She's fixing to put Ruby Day back in the Henry R. Mason Home for the Feebleminded."

"I heard you the first time, Luna," Daddy said. "But I just don't know if there is anything we can or should do."

"Can you at least talk to the woman?" Mama asked. "Tell her that Ruby Day is doing fine. That Luna is moved in and helping."

Daddy twisted his mouth and scratched behind his ear. "I guess I can try. But I can't guarantee she'll listen. And why should she?"

"Sapphire is coming back on Tuesday," I said. "Isn't there some way we can stop her? I mean, besides just talking to her, because Aunt Sapphire is a force, kind of like a mountain."

"Jesus can move mountains," Mama said.

Daddy rubbed his head like he was thinking and then said, "Just don't go, Ruby Day. Maybe you should hunker down and say flat out *no*. Like you mean it."

Ruby Day shook her head—hard.

I grabbed her hand. "Ruby Day, I think there is something you're not telling us."

She shook harder. And that was when I dashed over to the coat closet and got that envelope I found. I didn't know if it had anything to do with Ruby Day's problem, but it looked so official.

"What you got there, Luna?" Daddy asked.

I watched Ruby Day's eyes grow wide. She swallowed like she was swallowing a rhinoceros. "Whatever this is, Ruby Day," I said, "I'll fix it."

Daddy opened the envelope and took out a thick piece of paper folded into three equal sections. "Maybe you can't," Daddy said, holding the paper so I could see. The word *DEED*, in big black letters, stared me in the face.

CHAPTER
15

I held my breath.

"Go on, Justus," Mama said. "What's it say?"

Daddy cleared his throat. He looked first at Mama, then me, and finally at Ruby Day. "Did you know about this all the time, Ruby Day?" he asked.

Ruby Day pouted and blinked.

"What is it, Daddy? What's it say?"

"It says that Sapphire Whitaker is the owner of Ruby Day's house."

That tore it. Ruby Day punched her head and wailed like a banshee. She wailed so loud that April and June and Jasper came running inside.

"What's wrong? Did someone else die?" Jasper called.

Mama jumped up faster than a jack-in-the-box

clown and shuttled my brother and sisters outside. "Get on now. Nobody died. But it does seem that little garter isn't the only snake in town."

The twins pressed their noses against the porch window until Daddy saw them. All he had to do was *pretend* to stand up and those girls bolted a mile down the road.

"So what?" I said. "So what if Aunt Sapphire owns the house? It's still Ruby Day's."

Daddy shook his head. "Luna Fish, it means Sapphire can force Ruby Day out if she wants, or she can just up and sell it right out from under Ruby Day."

My heart pounded. "No. That's not fair. Why would she do that?"

"We don't know," Mama said. "But there is obviously some reason this Sapphire woman wants Ruby Day to go back to that dreadful hospital."

I watched Ruby Day's face turn as red as a Radio Flyer wagon. "Mason told me he was fixin' to buy my house when he got older. Buy it right out from under Sapphire."

"So Mason knew all along?" I said. "I bet he taped the deed under the lid. In case he needed it someday."

Ruby Day tilted her head at me like she did when she didn't understand, or when she was really sorry about something.

"Mason knew about Sapphire?" I said.

She cried, and I cried with her.

That was when Mama got her dander up. She stood with both fists on the table. "There must be something we can do. Some way to fight this, Justus."

Daddy folded the deed back into its three equal sections and stuffed it back inside the envelope. "Can't fight a legal document."

"Then we'll move," I said. "Ruby Day and I will get another place to live."

"You are still in school and not old enough to get a place, Luna," Mama said. "And Ruby Day certainly does not make enough money to support a household."

"Oh, Mama, we can't let Sapphire take her back. We can't."

"Family," Daddy said. "You can't fight family ties."

Mama sat back down and helped herself to another helping of chocolate pudding. She put some in Ruby Day's bowl, but Ruby Day pushed it away.

"I can't help but think that that woman has an ulterior motive," Mama said. "Something else is going on. I can feel it in my chest."

I felt the same ugly feeling in my chest. I just didn't know how to express it except to say, "I think you're right, Mama. Something is not right about this whole thing."

Daddy finished his pudding and set his bowl on the end table. He stretched and laid his head back.

"Will you think on it, Daddy?" I asked. "Think about talking to Sapphire. Maybe get to the truth?"

"God has the answer, Luna Fish. It might not be the one we're looking for, but he has the answer."

"That's right," Mama said. "If Ruby Day is meant to stay, she will. Even Aunt Sapphire isn't stronger than God."

Ruby Day swallowed several times, like something sour was stuck in her throat.

"Mama," I said. "Would you mind terribly if I didn't help wash the dishes and just took Ruby Day home?"

"That's fine. You take her home and Daddy and me will think on it. We will."

Ordinarily, Ruby Day would have been out in her garden on such a pretty fall day. She liked to rake the leaves into a big pile. Mason used to help her and we would always take running, leaping, flying, head-first jumps into the pile. Then we'd laugh and rake them again. Mason liked to burn them. He would turn up his jazz records, especially Rosemary Clooney singing "Autumn Leaves," while they burned.

But that day, the leaves were left to blanket the back-yard. An occasional gust swirled them around like they were being mixed by a great big spoon. Ruby Day and I sat in the kitchen for a long, long time.

"You sure you don't want to rake the leaves?" I asked.

"Not today, Luna."

"Want a cup of tea?"

"No, thank you, Luna."

Suddenly it seemed like the best thing that could happen would be for Tuesday to come.

"Maybe I should get my suitcase, Luna. Put my clothes inside."

"Ruby Day, don't even say that. We still got all of tomorrow to get through. We'll think of something. Daddy said God has the answer. Let's just wait."

"Okay, Luna."

"Did you hate the hospital?" I asked.

"Yes. But ... not Jeb. I didn't hate him."

"You mean Mason's father?"

Ruby Day's bottom lip started to quiver. "Yes. Mason's daddy." She fiddled with the saltshaker. "He used to be my husband."

I pulled Ruby Day close. "I'm sorry. I'm sure you miss him."

She pulled back and wiped her eyes under her glasses. "Everybody dies. Don't die, Luna."

"I won't."

We stayed quiet for a couple more minutes, and then Ruby Day got up and headed for the dining room and the shoebox. She dumped the pictures out onto the floor. They scattered just like the leaves outside. She shuffled through the pile until she found what she was looking for.

"Him," she said. "Jeb."

I took the picture of a tall, lanky man with close-cut hair and big eyes behind thick lenses who stood next to the Henry R. Mason Home for the Feebleminded sign.

"Did you get married at the hospital?"

"Yes," Ruby Day said. "But only for"—she counted on her fingers—"six, seven, eight—a little while. Jeb died." She snuffed snot down the back of her throat and wiped tears from her cheek.

"I'm sorry. I really am."

It was impossible for me to imagine what Ruby Day felt. I only knew how sad I was when Mason died. It was double for her. And now she was on the verge of losing her home.

CHAPTER
16

The next morning, Monday, Ruby Day ate her breakfast—Cheerios with milk and a sliced banana. She dressed for work like it was any ordinary day.

"Ruby Day," I said as I sliced a banana into my own cereal. "Are you sure you want to go to work this morning?"

She nodded. "I got to go, Luna. It's my job."

"I guess you'll need to talk to Mr. Haskell. Tell him about Sapphire."

Ruby Day didn't say anything for what felt like ten whole minutes, but I knew it was just a few seconds. "I . . . I don't know what to tell him."

"Just tell him the truth." I swallowed a mouthful of Cheerios.

Tears formed in Ruby Day's eyes. She whipped her glasses off and rubbed her face until it looked like a red apple.

"Now you stop it, Ruby Day," I said. I took her hands. "I'm just saying you should tell him in case ... in case I can't find a way to stop Sapphire from taking you back with her, but ... I will. You'll see."

Ruby Day pushed her cereal bowl away from her. She put her glasses on and stood up. "I need to get to work. Will you come with me?"

"Me? But I have school and ..."

"Please, Luna. You can tell Mr. Haskell better than me."

I sucked a breath through my nose. "Okay. I'll go. I'll just call school and tell them I'm going to be a little late."

I watched Ruby Day punch in her time card and tie her Haskell's Grocery Store apron around her waist. "He ain't here yet," she said. "I don't see his coat or hat on the hooks."

That was when Lavinia popped her head into the break room. "Morning, Ruby Day. Morning, Luna."

We said "Good morning, Lavinia" together.

"What's wrong?" Lavinia asked. "How come you look so sad, Ruby Day?"

"Aunt Sapphire come to take me back," Ruby Day said.

By now Lavinia was all the way in the break room and standing just a couple feet away from Ruby Day. "What?" She looked at me.

"Ruby Day's aunt wants her to move back to Philadelphia with her."

Lavinia's brown eyes grew about as big as bottle caps. "How come?"

I explained the best I could without going into too much detail. I figured it wasn't any of Lavinia's business that Sapphire was really planning on having Ruby Day sent back to the Home for the Feebleminded.

"Why, that's just awful," Lavinia said. "Imagine that. How come you're gonna let her, Luna? Can't you stop her?"

"I'm trying," I said. "But I can't figure out how—exactly."

"Well there must be something," Lavinia said. She put her hand on Ruby Day's shoulder. "It ain't right."

Ruby Day started to shake a little and Lavinia pulled her close. Lavinia looked over at me. "I got a feeling there's more than meets the eye going on. I can tell about these things sometimes. I have a sinking feeling in my guts."

"You and me and Mama," I said. "We all have a bad feeling, but we don't know why, not yet anyway."

Ruby Day rubbed her eyes just as Mr. Haskell walked into the break room. "What's going on, ladies? We got customers out there looking for a checker."

"Sorry, Mr. Haskell," Lavinia said. "I'll get right out there."

He hung up his coat and hat. "Anything wrong?"

I told Mr. Haskell the same thing I told Lavinia.

He said the same thing everybody had said. "That's not right." But even Mr. Haskell had no ideas about stopping it.

"You don't have to work today, Ruby Day," he said. "Seeing how you're leaving tomorrow. Wish I'd known. I'd have given you a proper send-off—you know, a party."

"No, thank you," Ruby Day said, and she headed toward the cash register as if bagging canned beans and briskets was the most important thing in the world.

I stayed a few more minutes and talked with Mr. Haskell. But it just seemed the more we talked about the problem, the bigger it got. Finally I said, "I need to get to school."

Mr. Haskell nodded as he looked out into the store. "I hate to lose her. She's a good person, a good worker."

"Well, if I count my chickens right," I said, "she won't go."

At school that day I told everyone who would listen

about the situation. I told Mrs. Grady, Coach Trawler, and even Principal Saletsky. Nobody had an answer, and they all just kind of shrugged their shoulders and said, "What a shame."

I could hardly concentrate on my schoolwork all day and was never so glad to get home. Ruby Day's shoebox was still on the dining room table, everything jumbled from being dumped out so many times. I decided to look through the pictures again, hoping to find something that would change the course of events. Nothing new. Nothing different. No answers. I did find a picture of a man wearing a hat, a gray suit, and white shirt with a black bowtie, and he was standing near a car—a very old car. I wondered if he was Ruby Day's grandfather or maybe Uncle Charles.

Five o'clock rolled around and Ruby Day had still not come home from work. My heart raced every time I stepped out on the porch looking for her. Where could she be? I waited on the porch, thinking how terrible it must be for her. I could see her crouching like she did on her heels, crying and rocking. Rocking and crying.

The five twenty-three bus pulled up to the curb. *Please, Lord, let her be on this one. It's getting dark.* I didn't like the idea of Ruby Day being out that late. Relief filled my heart when I saw her step onto the curb. She stopped a second and waved to the driver just like she always did.

"Ruby Day," I called. "I was worried about you."

"Don't be worried, Luna," she called back. Then she walked to the porch before saying anything else.

"I went to . . . to say good-bye to Mason."

"Oh, I should have thought of that. But I wish I had known. I would have gone with you."

She shook her head. "No, Luna, I wanted to go by myself, like after Daddy died, before I moved here. Uncle Charles drove me to the cemetery but I said good-bye by myself."

"I understand," I said. I opened the screen door and we went inside, and that was when it dawned on me.

"Uncle Charles?" I said. "Is this him?" I showed her the picture I saw. "He looks nice."

Ruby Day removed her hat and coat and hung them on the coat rack. She laughed. "Yep, Uncle Charles. He helped my daddy with things."

"Was he Aunt Sapphire's husband?"

Ruby Day laughed so hard she grabbed her stomach. "No. Just Daddy's friend."

I still didn't quite get it, but I supposed it didn't matter.

CHAPTER
17

Tuesday arrived cold and blustery. I woke around seven o'clock and couldn't find Ruby Day anywhere in the house. I searched every room. I went through the kitchen to the garden thinking she must be there, tending to her flowers. Ruby Day grew beautiful yellow and orange mums in fall, and I wouldn't put it past her to want to say good-bye to her garden. But she wasn't there.

I started to get a little scared that maybe she'd run off, or worse—maybe Aunt Sapphire came back in the night and took her, just took her like she was nothing more than a doll baby on a shelf.

"Mama," I said to myself. "I better call Mama."

But then I heard Ruby Day calling me from outside. I pulled open the front door and pushed open the screen. Ruby Day had put on her heavy wool coat and wrapped a long red scarf around her neck. Her yellow knit hat was pulled down over her ears. She was clutching the porch post like someone onboard a ship in a stormy sea, hanging on for dear life as the waves rolled and the winds whipped around her.

"Ruby Day, what are you doing out there? It's cold. You'll blow away in this wind."

"Don't want to go," she said.

"I know, but you can't stay out here. You can't cling to that post forever."

"Can too, Luna. I can stay here."

"But we're not even sure what time Sapphire is coming back. Come inside and wait." I shivered against the cold. "Please. Come inside."

Ruby Day shook her head. "No."

"Okay, but don't go anywhere else. Just stay on the porch."

I ran to the kitchen and was just about to call Mama when the telephone rang. It was Mr. Haskell.

"Morning, Luna," he said. "I wanted to check on Ruby Day. Is she okay? Did Sapphire come back for her?"

I hesitated for a few seconds. "Not yet," I said. "And yes, sir, she's all right—mostly. But you see, she's hanging on the porch post and won't let go on account of she doesn't want to go back to Philadelphia."

The receiver went silent.

"Mr. Haskell?" I said.

I heard him chuckle and that made me kind of mad. "How come you're laughing?"

"I'm sorry," he said. "But that sounds like Ruby Day. She can be stubborn. Sapphire might have to take her to Philly attached to the house."

"I just hope I can stop her," I said.

Next, I called my school and told the secretary, Mrs. Swanson, that I wouldn't be coming in. She didn't care as much as Mr. Haskell.

"Now, Luna," she said. "You can't stay home from school because Ruby Day is refusing to go home."

"I didn't say *home*," I said into the phone with my voice getting screechy. "I said THE HOME—for the feebleminded. It's a terrible place."

"You'll need a note from your mother," was all she said. "But I'll tell your teacher."

I went back to the porch. Ruby Day was still hanging on for dear life, it seemed.

"Ruby Day, please come back inside."

"No." Her face and hands were bright red. She looked uncomfortable and tired like she hadn't slept all night, and her eyes kept threatening to close. I felt I had no other choice but to let her stand there until she grew tired enough to come inside. Finally, an hour later she did. There was still no sign of Aunt Sapphire, and so I sent Ruby Day to bed while I tried to figure out what to do.

It was three o'clock in the afternoon before Ruby Day woke up and came to the living room, and I still hadn't thought of a solution. I sat on the couch with my head in my hands. "There must be some way. Some way to stop this. If only Uncle Charles were here. You said he helped your daddy. Maybe he can help you."

"Uncle Charles," Ruby Day said. "He wrote me a letter."

"A letter? Really? Where is it?"

I wanted to see this letter, but before I could ask, Ruby Day jumped up as though a firecracker went off under her bottom, and she ran up the steps. She had a sloppy way of running, and I thought she might trip and fall. "I'll get it, Luna," she said. "My letter."

"Here you go, Luna." She handed me an envelope. The writing on the outside was the same as the lettering on the other envelope. The one with the deed inside. I worried that I was holding nothing but bad news in my hand.

"It's from Uncle Charles," Ruby Day said.

I pulled a sheet of paper from the envelope and unfolded it. I started to read, and once I got to the end I could hardly believe my eyes.

"Ruby Day," I said. "You knew this all along?"

But just then I heard a car pull into the driveway.

"Aunt Sapphire," said Ruby Day, and she dashed back out the door. I followed. Ruby Day resumed her grasp on the porch post, and I stood there next to her holding the letter in my hand as we watched Aunt Sapphire's fancy car come to a stop.

CHAPTER
18

I watched Aunt Sapphire's chauffeur help her out of the backseat.

"Thank you, Frederick. I won't be too long. You should wait in the car."

Frederick tipped his cap. "Very good, Ma'am." And he closed the door with a bang.

Aunt Sapphire flung her dead foxes around her shoulders and harrumphed toward us.

"Hellooo, Aunt Sapphire," Ruby Day called. I knew she was trying to be strong and courageous and steadfast.

I didn't want to be so polite and only waved. I kept looking at the letter.

Sapphire walked up the porch steps. Her tiny heels clicked like crickets.

"I hope you're packed, Ruby Day," Sapphire said. "It's a long ride home."

"She's not," I said. "Ruby Day has decided to stay." I waved the letter in the air.

"Nonsense," Aunt Sapphire said. Then she looked at Ruby Day. "And why are you hanging onto that … that pole?"

Ruby Day didn't say a word. She just pressed in tighter with her cheek against the post.

"I told you," I said. "She isn't budging. And I guess you don't know about this." I waved the letter a second time.

Sapphire started to stutter and bluster. "Why … why she must move. She can't stay here. Not now. And who are you to tell me what—and what have you got there, young lady?"

"It's a letter from Uncle Charles."

"Charles? You mean Charles Radcliffe?"

I looked at the letter. On top, in fancy writing, it read *Radcliffe, Porter, and Tremanian—Attorneys at Law.* "I suppose so. But Ruby Day just knows him as Uncle Charles."

I thought Aunt Sapphire was going to fall right back down the porch steps. She teetered and tottered on her heels, her foxes flailing like the skinny, gutless creatures they were, until she regained her composure. The foxes sure didn't have any backbone, and I hoped I could find mine.

"What?" Sapphire said. "Show me that letter. This instant, young lady."

"No." I took a step back. "And you can't take Ruby Day back to the Henry R. Mason Home for the Feebleminded. Not when we know the truth. This letter will stop you. It tells the truth about you."

Aunt Sapphire tried to pull Ruby Day from the post. "Come on, dear. You know this is best. It doesn't matter what's in that letter. You must do as I say. I am your guardian."

"No. You aren't," I said. "According to this letter you're just ... just the third person in line for Mason's money ... I think."

"Oh, yes, Mason. Poor soul. Would have been better if we put him up for adoption like we wanted."

"Adoption?" I said. "You tried to take Mason away from Ruby Day?"

Sapphire sucked in a breath and blew it out like a bull. It smelled like old coffee and licorice. "Oh, dear, yes, of course we did. The pour soul would have been better off."

"He was not a poor soul. Never was, never will be. He always said he was richer than most and had more to be happy about. I just never knew how rich." I stamped my foot on the porch floor. "You are just such a ..."

"Careful, young lady," she said. "Respect your elders." She glared at me. It sent a chill down my spine.

"Come with me, Ruby Day," Sapphire said. "You don't need to pack. I'll buy you all brand-new clothes when we get home. New dresses. New shoes. Everything you need. Brand new."

Sapphire tried to pry Ruby Day's arms from the post.

"I wouldn't do that if I were you," I said. "She might start to wail."

"Nonsense. Come now, Ruby Day," Aunt Sapphire said. "We need to leave. I gave you plenty of time."

"No," Ruby Day said. "I ain't going back."

"But you must."

"Nope." And then she started to wail louder than I had ever heard her wail before. Only this time I cheered her on.

Sapphire looked so unnerved she let go of Ruby Day. "Well this is just preposterous."

"And you are just . . . just ostentatious," I said.

"I must use your telephone." Sapphire looked toward the front door. "You *do* still have a telephone, correct? I know I had one installed."

I bowed and waved low with a sweep of my hand, secretly hoping the time it took for her to make her call would be time enough to make a plan. "Of course. It's in the kitchen."

I opened the screen door for her. "It's the black thing on the wall in the kitchen."

That was when I caught Frederick's eye. He looked away. Like he was in on the whole thing too.

I sat on the steps and started to think. "There must be a way to make her just drive away and leave us alone," I said. Then I saw my sister Delores, of all people, marching up the driveway lugging a suitcase.

"Luna Fish," she called. "Can I stay with you and Ruby Day?"

"Delores? Do you have any idea what is going on? And why are you asking me that *now*?"

Delores stopped when she got to the Plymouth. "Who's fancy chariot is this?" she said with her voice all flouncy like anyone cared. "It's the ginchiest—like, wowsville."

I hated it when Delores talked like that. Like she was so hip and all.

"It's Aunt Sapphire's. Haven't you heard?" Then I remembered that she went to Carl's for Sunday supper.

"She's here to take Ruby Day back to the Home for the Feebleminded, and I'm trying to stop her."

"Aunt Sapphire? What a name. She sounds real cool."

"No, she isn't," I said. "She's … she's ostentatious. And didn't you hear what I just said?"

"Oh, why are you always the bearer of bad news? Anybody with a chauffeur has got to be the coolest."

Delores dropped her ratty old suitcase on the pavement. "Where is she? And why in the world is Ruby Day hanging onto that post and crying?"

"She doesn't want to go."

"Go where?"

"I just told you, Delores. Back to the home. It's a bad place. A place where they hurt people like Ruby Day. Mama said so."

"But maybe it would be best for her, Luna. You can't live with her ... forever."

"Yes I can. That's my plan. I'll go to college and become a teacher and take care of myself and Ruby Day."

"Suit yourself. But it sounds like a dumb idea."

Delores started up the porch steps. "I want to meet Aunt Sapphire — wow, what a name. With a name like Sapphire, she could be one of them silent screen stars."

"She's not," I said. "And how come you came here with a suitcase? Did Daddy finally toss you out?"

"No." Delores put her hands on her hips and when she did both of her knee-high socks drooped down to her ankles in sloppy wrinkles. "He got mad on account of I was kissing Carl on the stump in the backyard. So ... I left. I told him I am fifteen years old. Old enough to kiss a boy."

I had a feeling there was more to the story than that, but it would have to keep for another time.

"Mama was just seventeen when she married Daddy," Delores said.

"This isn't the time to settle your silly problems. We have to help Ruby Day."

Delores moved closer to me and whispered in my

ear. "I still say it's better this way. You know she is . . . retarded."

"She's smarter than you," I said. "Maybe we should send you to a home for the . . . incurably selfish. And never use that disgusting word."

I heard Frederick laugh.

"Don't be so mean, Luna. I am not acting selfish. Now I want to see Aunt Sapphire. Where is she?"

"Inside. Talking on the telephone—leastways that's what she said."

Delores pulled open the screen door and went inside.

"Don't you worry about Delores, Ruby Day. You keep hanging onto your porch post."

"Okay, Luna. I will."

I stood next to Ruby Day, my heart pounding like a big brass drum, though I didn't tell Ruby Day that. I had to use the information in the letter to stop Aunt Sapphire. But how?

CHAPTER
19

The wind settled down a little but the air was still cold. Dark clouds had moved in overhead, and I prayed that God would not send rain that day. We had enough storms for one season. Then Delores pushed open the screen door.

"Luna, Luna!" she said. "I got to tell you something."

"Not now, Delores."

"No, it's about Sapphire and Ruby Day. It's important."

I let go of the post. "What?"

"I heard her on the telephone. I was standing in the dining room waiting—you know I didn't want to interrupt her while she was talking on the phone. So I stood there and well, I couldn't help but overhear—"

"What? What did you hear?"

Delores caught her breath. "I heard her tell whoever it was on the other end that if she didn't find a way to get Ruby Day back then Ruby Day would get to keep all her money."

"I know all about it," I said. I waved the letter toward her. "It's all in here."

"So you know about Mason's money," Delores said. "She mentioned a will and something about provisions—whatever that means."

Ruby Day wailed.

"Stop that this instant," Delores said. "A person can't even hear herself think over that shrieking. So you just hold on, Ruby Day. Just 'cause you're ... you know, slower than most, don't mean we have to listen to that noise."

"Delores," I said. "Don't talk to her like that."

"Well, if she wants to be treated like everyone else in the world, she'll need to learn to take it."

Ruby Day stopped her wailing, and I will confess that I was thankful Delores acted so stern.

"Listen, Delores," I said. "Go get Daddy and Mama." I thought for a second. "And anybody else you can think of."

"Okay, Luna, but—"

"No buts, just go. And hey—did Sapphire see you?"

Delores shook her head. "I don't think so, but ... boy, is she spectacular. Did you catch a load of them foxes she's wearing?"

"Just go," I said.

Delores ran down the driveway.

Ruby Day started to shake. I tried to hold on to her but it was like she just melted into a puddle on the porch, with her arms still wrapped around the post. I thought I might cry—but I remembered I needed to be strong and courageous and face the Sapphire storm head on.

That was when Sapphire came outside. Only this time she tried being so sickeningly sweet I thought I might upchuck.

"Ruby Day, darling," Sapphire said as she stroked Ruby Day's arm and helped her to her feet. "We only want what's best for you. Now please don't make me get ... well, *forceful* about it. You do remember that I own this house."

Ruby Day clung tighter. Her face was as bright red as a candy apple.

Sapphire tried once more to pry Ruby Day's arms from around the post.

"You can't force her," I said.

"You keep quiet," Sapphire said. "You're just a child. You have no say in this matter."

"That child is my daughter."

I looked up and saw Daddy standing near the Plymouth.

"You can't talk to my daughter like that." He walked toward Sapphire.

"Aunt Sapphire, I presume," Daddy said.

"Why yes, yes, I am."

"Justus T. Gleason. Luna's father."

Sapphire stepped away from Ruby Day. "Well, I am very glad to make your acquaintance, but you must realize, sir, that you have no say in this matter either. It's a ... family situation."

"I was hoping you would be reasonable," Daddy said. "And see it from Ruby Day's perspective. She likes it here. She visits Mason's grave nearly every single day. She can't do that if she's back in Philadelphia."

"She won't need to. She'll forget. People like her don't have good memories."

"A mother never forgets her children," Daddy said. "No matter what their ... situation."

I saw Mama, Polly Dog, and Delores making their way up the driveway. The big guns had arrived.

Daddy looked at me. "Now what's this about a letter? Delores was talking so fast. Something about a will?"

I handed Daddy the letter. "Go on, read it," I said. "It explains everything. Mason's granddaddy was a rich man, and he left nearly all his money to Mason, but Mason wouldn't get it until he turned sixteen."

Daddy read the letter. Then he looked at Sapphire. "I get it. According to this letter from the grandfather's lawyer, if for some reason Mason can't take the money then it goes to Ruby Day."

"Well, I hardly think this is any of your—"

"Unless," Daddy said, "Ruby Day is declared unfit and sent back to the home. Then you can control the money. Isn't that right, Sapphire?"

"That's right, Daddy," I said. "That's what I figured out. It was a big puzzle, but I knew she was up to no good. I'm just glad Ruby Day remembered the letter."

Aunt Sapphire glared into my face. I thought if her eyes were ray guns, I'd be dead.

"Oh, I can't believe this," Mama said. She pulled me in for a hug. "I am so glad you came to live with Ruby Day, Luna. I am so proud of you for sticking to your guns and getting to the truth."

"Uncle Charles said he would take care of me," Ruby Day said. "He told me not to worry."

"That's right," hollered Delores. "I heard Sapphire talking on the telephone."

For the first time, Delores's eavesdropping was welcome.

"That's right," I said. "Delores heard you say that if Ruby Day didn't go back to that ... that prison, then she'd get all the money."

Sapphire stuttered like a stuck fan blade. "But ... but it is none of your business. Why do you all care so much anyway?"

I saw Mr. Haskell coming up the driveway. He was followed by three other store employees and some of our neighbors. And then I couldn't hardly believe what

I saw next. The high school football team was coming down the road, led by Coach Trawler. I figured they really didn't want to be there, but Coach Trawler had a way of getting them boys to do what he wanted.

"Well, look at that," Daddy said. "The whole town is coming."

"I sent Jasper and the twins to round everyone up," Delores said.

"Why don't you try and explain matters, Sapphire?" Mama said. She took Sapphire's arm and directed her toward the front door. "Come inside and tell me the truth."

Sapphire jerked her arm away. "The truth is, my dear lady, that Ruby Day is a feebleminded idiot and needs more care than ... than that little girl can give."

I watched Mama pull herself up to her full height. "I'll have you know, *my dear lady*, that Luna Gleason is one of the most capable young ladies you'll ever have the pleasure of knowing. Ruby Day could not be in better hands, so how dare you call her that ... that despicable name."

Polly barked and snarled at Sapphire. I patted Polly's head, and when I did I spied April near the car. She was dangling a snake in one hand and trying to open the car door with the other. I knew what she was fixing to do, and I was truly going to tell her not to when Ruby Day wailed. She let go of the post and took a step toward Sapphire. Daddy held on to Ruby Day's hand. "Stay," he said.

"She is not an idiot," I said. "Ruby Day is smarter than a lot of people. She takes good care of her flowers, and she took good care of Mason and — "

"She's an excellent employee," Mr. Haskell said.

"She's never late," said Lavinia. "She's ... she's my friend."

"And we like her," said April and June.

"Yeah," said Jasper.

"This ... this display is ... is well, it won't get you anywhere. I'll just sell the house."

"Go ahead," said Daddy. "You still won't get Mason's money, and Ruby Day will buy her own house."

That made me cheer. "That's right. Ruby Day doesn't need you or your house or your stupid Home for the Feebleminded. Her home is right here. With me — " I looked over the crowd. "With us."

"Maybe you should just get back into your fancy-dancy car," Mama said, "and go back to your fancy-dancy house in Philadelphia — "

"Bryn Mawr," Sapphire said with her nose in the air.

"And leave Ruby Day's care to us." Mama indicated the now growing crowd on the street. "We'll all be taking care of her."

Ruby Day cried. "I ... I don't need money. I got a job, Aunt Sapphire."

"It's not enough, and you can't work forever,"

Sapphire said. "Now, don't you want to go back to Mason's Home? The place where you and Jeb got married? The place where Mason was born? I got a nice, pretty room all set up for you with flowers—your favorites. Lupines and mums."

"Lupines don't bloom in fall," Ruby Day said. "I am smart."

"Then we'll get them in spring." Sapphire's voice dripped with so much molasses I nearly slipped in the driveway.

Frederick walked toward the porch. "You silly, silly people do not understand. Sapphire is more capable of knowing what's best for this poor, wretched woman then any of you. *She,* after all, is family."

"No," I said. "I'm her family."

"Silly girl," Frederick said.

"I bet he's in on it too," Lavinia said. "He has cagey eyes."

Sapphire walked onto the porch and stood in front of Ruby Day. "Now look, honey, just get in the car. I have your favorite chocolate bars in there and a bouquet of roses right in the backseat. You want to see the roses?"

I felt glued to the driveway when I heard Ruby Day say, "Yes, Aunt Sapphire. I love to look at pretty flowers." I could hardly believe it as I watched Sapphire lead Ruby Day toward the car.

"No! Ruby Day, don't go!" I hollered. "Don't get in her car."

"I just want to see the roses," Ruby Day said.

"Please," I called. I started after her. I managed to grab her coat sleeve but Sapphire yanked my arm away. "You let her be!"

"Ruby Day," I called. "Run inside the house."

"And you can have that chocolate," said Aunt Sapphire. "I'll buy you lots more too."

"Don't go, Ruby Day," Delores called. "She doesn't care about you."

Frederick opened the back door.

"Daddy," I said. "Do something."

Daddy shook his head. "Luna, I don't agree, but I can't stop them either. Maybe that Uncle Charles can help down the road, but for now—"

The next thing I knew, Ruby Day had climbed into the backseat and Sapphire climbed in after her. She slammed the door shut.

I ran toward the car. "Ruby Day. No." I pulled on the door but it was locked.

Delores put her arm around me. "I don't believe it. She got in the car."

Frederick got in the driver's seat, and I heard the engine start. My heart raced along with it.

I took Delores's hand and pulled her toward the Plymouth. "Lay down," I said. "Like this." I stretched out as close as I could to the back wheels of Sapphire's car.

Daddy banged on Frederick's window. "Don't back up. My daughter's there."

"What are you doing?" I heard Frederick holler.

I shut my eyes tight and held Delores's hand. Then I heard the car door open and a second later Sapphire stood over me like some shadowy monster. The dark clouds drifted behind her.

"Get up from there this instant," Sapphire said.

"I will not," I said. "Frederick can run over me if he wants, but I'm not giving up."

Polly Dog skittered by and lay down at my feet. She whimpered and then looked at me with her bright eyes.

"Well, if that's what you want," Sapphire said.

I heard her click back to the car door and a second later the car door closed.

"Luna, what are you doing?" Daddy called.

"Don't you get it, Justus?" Mama said. "She's laying down her life. For her friend."

Mama lay down next to Delores and held her hand. Then the twins and Jasper lay down on the ground. Then Mr. Haskell, and before I could say Jack Robinson the football team and Coach Trawler had joined the chain along with everyone else who was there. Even Clovis Hunkle, the boy Coach pulled out of Mason's funeral, lay down in the street.

"I'm doing it for Mason," Clovis said. "I ... I'm sorry I made fun of Miss Ruby Day."

"We can't let you take Ruby Day," I hollered.

"That's right," Daddy said. He squeezed next to Mama and me. "I'm proud of you, Luna, for caring so much about Ruby Day. I'm sorry I doubted you. I'm sorry I doubted your strength."

I squeezed Daddy's hand.

I closed my eyes tight to keep tears from spilling. When I opened them I saw Aunt Sapphire standing over me once again. A great dark cloud passed right behind her.

"You win. For now," Aunt Sapphire said. "But I'll be keeping my eye on you."

"Go ahead," Mama said. "Luna and Ruby Day will be just fine. We're all watching."

Thanksgiving arrived a couple of weeks after the Aunt Sapphire incident. Mama, of course, invited Ruby Day and me over for Thanksgiving Day dinner. Delores and Daddy had settled their squabble, and she and Carl made plans to become engaged when Delores turned seventeen, in spite of Daddy's protests.

As a result, the table that year was fuller than it had ever been. Mama made the traditional foods — turkey with stuffing, and mashed potatoes that were so creamy and tasty I could have eaten them for days. Delores's favorite was dessert, but she was so sweet on Carl she hardly ate anything. Ruby Day especially liked yams with marshmallows. And Daddy, of course, stood at the head of the table and carved the bird.

"Before Daddy asks the blessing," I said, "I got something to say."

"What is it, Luna?" Mama asked.

"You all know how I always wanted to be a teacher. Well now I know what kind of teacher. I'm going to become one of them special teachers that teach kids with . . . kids like Ruby Day."

Mama took a deep breath. "Why, Luna, I think that's wonderful."

"Thank you, Mama. I don't know how exactly, but maybe I can help. Maybe I can help people understand that folks like Ruby Day aren't feebleminded or retarded or any of the other silly words people make up."

Daddy pointed his finger at me. "Luna, I couldn't be more proud of you then I am right now. And you were right. You can do anything you set your mind and heart on."

After the blessing—which was longer than usual—hands went wild around the table as the food was served. Ruby Day's eyes lit up like Christmas tree bulbs when she got her first taste of Mama's homemade cranberry sauce.

"I have a question, Ruby Day," I said between bites. "I've been meaning to ask you but keep forgetting. How come you named your son Mason, if that was the name of that terrible hospital?"

Ruby Day swallowed. She smiled for a minute like

she was remembering something, or trying to recall something important.

"I remember," she said. She swallowed another bite of yams. "The sign in the picture gave me the idea, Luna."

Mama put her fork on her plate. "I think I understand. Ruby Day, did you decide to name him Mason after the hospital because it was a way to make a bad place good?"

Ruby Day smiled so wide the yams squeezed through her teeth.

"How'd you get so smart, Mama?" I asked.

"She married me," Daddy said.

"You can't take all the credit, Justus."

Jasper raised his milk glass. "I miss Mason."

"He's here," Ruby Day said. She pushed her chair back, stood up, and dashed out the front door.

"Where's she going?" Delores asked. "Shouldn't someone go after her?"

"Give her a minute," Mama said.

But I wasn't so sure if I should wait or run after her.

I pushed my chair back. Daddy grabbed my hand. "Wait, Luna Fish."

April looked at me and smiled. "Do you think that cranky lady found the snake I put in her car?"

Daddy laughed so hard he nearly choked. Mama shook her head. "April, you didn't."

Ruby Day dashed back into the house carrying Mason's picture right before April could confess.

"Where should I put it?" she asked.

Mama made a space on the crowded table between the mashed potatoes and the peas. "Right here, Ruby Day. Put Mason's picture right here."

"Is it all right to put a picture on the table?" Ruby Day asked.

"Ain't no rule," I said.

Daddy flipped on the hi-fi, and the notes of "Autumn Leaves" swirled and danced into the dining room.

Dear Reader,

I hope you enjoyed reading about Luna and her family. Luna was very brave to move in with Ruby Day after Mason died. She was also smart and truly showed what it means to consider someone else more highly than herself. She was brave to stand up to Aunt Sapphire. Sadly, many years ago, people with developmental delays like Ruby Day were often sent to live in institutions far away from their families and the "normal" public. That was what Aunt Sapphire wanted for Ruby Day.

Sometimes residents were taught their colors or how to read, but most of the time, society considered people with educational disabilities a burden. People with mental disabilities were not educated or taught a trade so they would be able to live on their own or become active, productive members of society. Often the residents of these professional institutions were forced to take care of the buildings, to clean the bathrooms and scrub the floors. Sometimes they were tranquilized so they could be kept under control. People like Ruby Day were called "morons," "idiots," "imbeciles," "retards," or, as in Ruby Day's case, "feebleminded"—these are terrible words that only harm God's precious children.

I got the idea to write this story after watching a documentary about the history of mental retardation and seeing the vivid and sometimes terrifying images of people in these institutions. Sometimes the institutions were called "homes." It broke my heart to see how human beings could be so misunderstood. I don't think the people in charge of these homes were mean-spirited or nasty. They just didn't know as much about educational delays as we know today. By the mid-1970s most of these institutions were closed, and the resident students were moved into the general community.

I wanted to write about someone who overcame all these obstacles. Ruby Day had a job she enjoyed, hobbies—like her garden—and she lived a productive, happy life with friends and family who loved her. Fortunately, children with developmental delays today usually stay with their families. My friend Christa has a daughter with Down's syndrome. Her name is Sarah. After she graduated from high school, Sarah went to live in a community with other adults just like her. Sarah has a job and an active social life. Her mom told me that sometimes she calls Sarah and Sarah doesn't even have time to talk to her. She's too busy working or talking with her friends.

Sometimes special-needs children go to different schools. If you look in the front of this book, you'll see that it is dedicated to my young friend Anna Halter. Anna has autism and is considered severely mentally disabled. She lives with her mom and dad and sister, but she goes to a school specially designed to work with students with disabilities. At Anna's school, she receives physical therapy to help improve the way her body moves. With help, Anna rides horses and learns to brush her teeth, set the table, and make her bed. She is also learning how to pay for things she might want to purchase. Anna goes home every day. She has not been shut away. She is being given opportunities to learn and grow to her potential. While I was writing *Carrying Mason*, Anna turned twenty, but she functions as an eighteen-month-old child. Anna will never be able to take care of herself or live in a community like Sarah, but she is home with her family where she is happiest.

At your school, you may have noticed some students get more help with their class work or might get called out from time to time to work with a special teacher. But that doesn't make him or her strange or unlikable. And that's a good thing. When we meet someone with an intellectual disability, we should see the person first, before the disability.

Blessings,
Joyce Magnin

We want to hear from you. Please send your comments about this
book to us in care of zreview@zondervan.com. Thank you.